I0763406

The Lost Forest Trilogy

Legacy of the Golden Bird

By

Lainey Miles

This book is dedicated to my family, especially my late mother, who was a true inspiration of strength, character, and her never-ending support and love for her family.

Acknowledgment

To my Aunt Geneva, who I admire greatly. I want to thank you for your invaluable input, advice, and encouragement.

Table of Contents

PROLOGUE

Under the House of Darkwick, the Helve Dynasty ruled the land centuries before the Royal Family of Pishtar appeared. During King Helve's reign, his subjects were brutally treated, resulting in the populace fearing him and his men. They denigrated people, beat them, heavily taxed them, and simply seized any goods by force, materials, crops, or livestock they desired.

In contrast, the Pishtars were humble and benevolent people who, throughout the generations, showed kindness to all inhabitants while carefully nurturing the surrounding forests. Unlike their predecessors, the Pishtars freely shared their wealth with all the less fortunate. Their compassion and generosity to all people throughout the land earned them admiration; hence, they were hailed royalty, and the Kingdom of the Meadow came into being. Thus, the House of Pishtar became the ruler of the land.

This change in ruling families naturally gave rise to a constant strife between the two forests. However, King Helve was not willing to be governed by anyone else, especially the Pishtars. Eventually, with the help of the Kingdom of the Meadow, the people revolted against the oppressive rule of the House of Darkwick, which forced King Helve to flee his territory.

Being driven out in shame, King Helve took his men and went deep into the darkest section of the forest, where he started the reign of terror all over again. Only the darkest, most evil factions are known to survive there; hence, it became known as The Dark Forest.

Among those who contributed to chasing King Helve out was the McDaniel family, who joined hands with the Pishtars to rid themselves of the Helve dynasty. By doing so, they became family friends and developed an unbreakable bond that lasted for centuries.

The fiercest McDaniel to come along was Charles John McDaniel, "Chuck," a descendant of the long line of mighty McDaniel warriors. He was a huge, powerful man and one of the fiercest warriors of his time. Known as Sir Charles, he had been knighted by King Sargon Pishtar of the Kingdom of the Meadow for his bravery in countless battles many years ago.

When quite young, Chuck used to sneak into his father's library, pull out old dusty books, and read ancient stories about famous warlords and brutal dictators. While rummaging about the library, he stumbled upon a rusty iron box that contained fascinating pictures and records of his ancestors. He knew he belonged to a fierce tribe of warriors, but he had never seen these pictures before. The records detailed the battles they fought in, the weapons they used, and even their strategies for the perfect battle outcome.

Chuck was fascinated by all of it, and as he grew older, his proficiency in this subject enabled him to become one of the greatest architects of the art of warfare. His knowledge and expertise led to his employment by Kings and Emperors alike, where he showed them how to plan and defeat their enemies. His devised schemes, complemented with proven battle strategies, were unlike anything any adversary had ever encountered.

Unfortunately, his reputation came with a price. Sensing their own mortality, the remaining tyrannical rulers came together. They had a bounty placed on Chuck's head – whoever killed the famous Sir Charles John McDaniel would be granted his own kingdom.

Aware that hundreds of men were on the hunt for Chuck, his fellow soldier, best friend, and Samurai, Oshiro Kehi, pleaded with Chuck to go underground and let things die down. Though reluctant, Chuck realized Kehi was right, so he agreed to leave. In the search for a new location, he had one place in mind—a secluded forest he had run across in his travels years ago. And so, Chuck, Kehi, and some trusted men set out. They followed Chuck deep into the forest without question.

Winding through the forest many days later, Chuck started getting frustrated. Even though this forest was beginning to look familiar, it still wasn't the place he remembered. Just when he was about to head in another direction, Chuck came across an enormous spider web, bigger than he had ever seen anywhere.

As he looked around, he felt this might be some sort of a trap because it was the only spider web they had encountered thus far. He thought it was odd not only for its size but also because the only thing caught in this web was a very tiny golden bird with a turquoise feathered ring around its neck. He knelt down to look closely at the tiny bird and saw that it wasn't moving. "Must be dead," he thought. He stood up and was about to leave when the tiny bird opened its eyes, stared at Chuck for a moment, and then let out a sorrowful sound.

Knowing he couldn't just leave this unusual bird here, he carefully untangled it, wrapped it up for warmth, and strapped it to his chest for protection. Little did Chuck know that the golden bird he just saved had been kidnapped from The Lost Forest.

Once he stood up to leave with his newfound friend, the unique opening to the forest he was searching for was right in front of him. A smile spread across Chuck's face. "Well, little one, we found our new home. This is it Kehi. Tell the men." And so, the building of the new fortress began.

The fortress, built primarily for security and privacy, was unique in its true sense. The edifice had been meticulously planned, just like the warfare expert would plan his battles. Its construction took several years and the most challenging architectural feat was persuading natural light to penetrate into the deepest underground passages. Yet, like all other seemingly impossible obstacles, that was also overcome. A deadly rushing river around the fortress capped off the last step of security. The end result was a work of art and beauty, all designed and engineered by Chuck himself, with the expert assistance of his great friend, Kehi, and, of course, his loyal men.

CHAPTER 1

"Are you sure this is the right place?" asked Salair, whispering.

"Yes, Salair, I am positive," answered Sasha.

"I'm worried! What if this is a trap Sasha?"

"Your father would never have sent us here if it were not the right place. Judging from his description, this has to be it," Sasha insisted. He stared at Salair and knocked on the door.

"But look at his place," implored Salair, seeing the cracked and warped boards on the broken shack before them. "This place looks like it will collapse at any moment."

Before Sasha had time to agree, the door opened just a crack. "Yes?" came a deep voice. "Uh, yes," Sasha was slightly leery but slipped a sealed envelope through the opening. "Hmmm," murmured the man, quickly glancing at the envelope and then back at Sasha. "One moment," he said and closed the door softly.

Sasha continued looking around to make sure no one had followed them. A few seconds later, the door reopened. "Please, come in at once." A tall, stout oriental man hurried them inside. He furtively peeked outside before shutting the door swiftly behind them.

"Thank you," Sasha managed to say as they were quickly ushered into an empty, dreary room containing a single thick iron door on the opposite wall.

The man crossed the room and pressed something on the door, which caused it to slide open. Before them was a dark elevator. "Please," he said while motioning them inside. Whispering something in Japanese, the elevator began its descent. He was silent the whole way down. Following his example, Salair and Sasha also stayed quiet.

The elevator jarred to a halt, and the doors slid open. "Please," the oriental man motioned for them to exit. Again, they stood in another dimly lit room with nowhere to go. Salair and Sasha exchanged nervous glances.

"Please wait here. I'll be right back," said the man as he left them to let Sir Charles know they had unexpected visitors. The oriental man was none other than Samurai Oshiro Kehi, Sir Charles' best friend.

"Of course," Sasha responded.

"Sasha, are you sure about this?" whispered Salair. "Maybe we have come to the wrong place."

"Your father's instructions were quite precise. He would never put you in danger."

"I know you're right. I just can't believe this is happening," Salair admitted as they silently waited.

While Kehi was busy tending to the uninvited guests, Chuck was, as usual, busy writing about his last battle. Like his ancestors, he wanted to document every fight so that the next generation could learn from it. He was out in his favorite spot, the Japanese garden – it was meticulously sculpted, containing bridges, bonsai trees, ponds teaming with rare koi fish, small waterfalls, and even a Japanese tea house (at Kehi's insistence). The river that flowed so violently around the fortress also entered the garden, but here, it was miraculously reduced to a leisurely bubbling brook. Indeed, it was a peaceful place.

"Excuse me, sir," interrupted Kehi, "but we have visitors."

"You're kidding, right Oshi?" Chuck laughed.

"No, I am not," replied Kehi while handing the Noble the note that Sasha had given him.

"Hmmm... I see," said Chuck, bolting upright, studying the scrap of paper. "This note is signed by my friend, the King."

"Yes, it is."

"You said guests... more than one?"

"Yes, two."

"Will you escort them into the great room please?"

"Of course!"

Kehi returned to the Princess and her Royal Guard. "Please accept my apologies for the guarded behavior. You are safe now. Follow me."

Sasha went first, keeping Salair behind him. Kehi stood in front of a wall, and again, he whispered something in Japanese, and immediately, an open door appeared. "This way please," he requested.

As they stepped through the door, they were awed by the fortress standing in front of their eyes.

"How is this even possible?" exclaimed Salair, approving of the intricate masonry of the fortress before her.

"Very impressive!" Sasha exclaimed.

"Thank you," replied Kehi. Then, getting down to business, he said, "This note is encrypted but signed by the King. How did you come by it?"

"The note is encrypted in case we were captured and had to talk our way out of something," answered Sasha. "This is Princess Salair of the Kingdom of the Meadow and King Pishtar's daughter of Queen Victoria and King Sargon of the House of Pishtar. I am Colonel Sasha Albion, head of the Royal Guards and bodyguard to the Princess. The King assured us Sir Charles would be here. I hope he was not mistaken?"

"No. Only the King would know of this location," the Samurai assured them. "I am Oshiro Kehi, Sir Charles' friend. I have informed him of your arrival. We'll meet him upstairs. Please follow me."

They crossed over the bridge, which hovered high above the moat. The sound of the roaring river was deafening. Guards on either side of the entrance opened the heavy iron doors.

"Please... " Kehi motioned them inside. They followed him along a path of intricately sculpted tiles. On the slightly darker side of the path ran a creek with elegant statues in the background. The lighter side was riddled with magnificently colored flowers. As they kept walking, their pathway became wider and brighter, leading them through a breathtaking tunnel lined with giant yellow English roses.

"My word!" exclaimed the Princess as she closed her eyes, inhaling the scent. "I have never seen English roses that huge. They are exquisite. This is truly baffling, Kehi. Aren't we underground?"

"Yes, we are," said Kehi with a satisfied smile on his face. "The roses are heirlooms passed down by Sir Charles' great-grandmother. Yes Princess, exquisite they are. This way please."

While making their way to the great room, the Princess stopped. "Is that a bird singing? If it is, I have never heard anything like that."

"Yes Princess, it is a bird. That is Berra. She must've sensed we have company. Would you like to see her? She's over this way."

Just ahead of them was Berra, perched on her favorite branch of an ancient Cherry tree. Berra, as Chuck had named her, was a rare golden eagle. Except for the circle of turquoise feathers outlining her neck, she was adorned in stunning gold feathers and pitch-black feet.

"What a beautiful bird. Her markings are quite remarkable. Have you ever seen anything like her Sasha?" asked the Princess as she stared at her.

"Not in my lifetime, Princess," said Sasha. Then turning towards the Samurai, he asked, "How did you come by this bird, Kehi?"

"On our travels to find this location, Sir Charles discovered her stuck in a giant spider web. She was just a baby then and probably would have died if we didn't stumble upon her. We have no idea how she got there. We think someone or something kidnapped her, but from where we don't know. We had this area built just for her. This is her favorite spot in the castle, and she regales us with highly unusual sounds and melodies. Sometimes, we think she may be calling out for her family. Some of her songs are quite sorrowful."

"That's quite sad. What a blessing Sir Charles happened upon her," commented Salair as she moved in to take a closer look at Berra. Glancing down at the Princess, Berra's turquoise feathers started glowing – it was unusual. As the Princess kept staring at Berra, her own eyes assumed a similar glow. This lasted a few seconds before the peculiar luminosity vanished.

“What in the world just happened?” asked an incredulous Sasha. “Did you see that Kehi?”

“I most certainly did. I have never seen Berra’s feathers glow,” exclaimed Kehi. “Salair, what was that? What happened?” asked Sasha.

“I’m not really sure, Sasha,” replied Salair, blinking her eyes frequently as if to come out of a trance. “That has never happened to me before. Something else was strange too.”

“What do you mean Princess?” asked Sasha.

“Well, a faint glimpse of a turquoise flower flashed in front of my eyes, and then it was gone. I don’t know what that would mean.”

“Maybe a vision of sorts, Salair?”

“Sounds like it,” said Kehi. “I have my doubts, but maybe Sir Charles would know about this phenomenon. If he doesn’t, this is significant without knowing what significance it has.” He looked a bit sheepish, then added, “I’m not even sure if that makes sense. Anyway, let’s get going and tell Sir Charles about this interesting development.”

Berra flew out of the tree and landed on Kehi’s shoulder as they continued on.

Salair wondered aloud, “How does sunlight come in here? We’re underground.”

Kehi avoided answering the question by vaguely stating, “One of the many nuances you will find in our fortress.”

They reached the end of the pathway and stood in front of a giant rock wall. "Here we are," announced Kehi. Leaning toward the wall, he once again chanted something in Japanese, and instantly, the wall folded into the ceiling, revealing a hidden staircase. Berra leaped off his shoulder and flew upstairs.

"This way, Princess."

"Oh my!" exulted the Princess as she ascended the staircase with Sasha and Kehi trailing behind. After going up several steps, she reached the top, which opened into a hallway leading to the main area. The hallway was lined with a collection of gleaming ancient swords with magnificent jewel hafts.

"Quite an impressive collection," Sasha murmured to the Princess.

"Yes, they are exquisite," agreed Salair.

"Some of these are quite old," Sasha continued. "These had to have been taken from royalty who perished while fighting, collected by someone in the same battle."

"Quite correct!" Sir Charles marched abruptly into the hallway from the main room to greet his guests. "And perish they did. Allow me to introduce myself." He politely bowed to the Princess. "I am Sir Charles McDaniel. I believe you are looking for me."

"Oh yes, we are...we were." The startled Princess carefully studied the man standing before her. Sir Charles proved to be quite handsome – large and muscular, with wide-set brown eyes, a Roman nose, and a strong chin, which fitted into a square attractive face – crowned with a beautiful mixture of thick black, tan, and brown hair.

"This is indeed an honor," stated Chuck. Intrigued by the Princess, Chuck made deliberate eye contact with Salair, who was staring at him.

Sasha interrupted the moment. “Ah, yes, but it is our honor, I’m sure,” extending his hand to Sir Charles as Kehi introduced them.

Sasha, the Commander of the Royal Guards of the Kingdom of the Meadow, was a tall, lean man with salt and pepper hair, maintaining an unmistakable toughness in his eyes. Captivated by her beauty, Sir Charles again switched his attention to the Princess. She was tall and fit, with ivory skin of perfection and thick blonde hair cascading down her back. The ends of her hair were black – very unusual. However, her most intriguing feature was her huge turquoise eyes. He could not keep from staring at her.

She lifted a graceful hand to him. “How do you do, Sir Charles? I apologize for the intrusion, but you have no idea how relieved we are to have found you.”

Accepting her proffered hand, Sir Charles remarked, “I have been the recipient of many intrusions before; believe me, this is the most welcome one. Please come in, and by the way, call me Chuck.”

“And I am Salair.”

He escorted them into the great room, which Salair thought should more appropriately have been referred to as the grand room—high walls of gleaming black marble with ancient tapestries, which looked more like priceless paintings, hung from the walls. Expensive antique furnishings filled the room, and on the back wall, a fireplace burnt brightly with suits of shining armor on either side.

“And I thought our palace was grand,” Salair whispered to Sasha. He readily agreed. “This is impressive.” The room gave them a tremendous sense of ease. He smiled to himself while glancing at Berra, who looked very regal as if she were the master of the house.

“Please make yourselves comfortable,” Chuck offered, gesturing them to be seated.

Seeing Sasha look at Berra caused Kehi to remember: "Chuck, before we continue, the most unusual thing just happened between the Princess and Berra."

"What do you mean?" Chuck inquired.

"The Princess and Berra seem to have something in common, which is highly unusual. Princess, if you don't mind... " Kehi motioned for her to approach Berra.

"Certainly." She stood and walked over to Berra's perch. They stared into each other's eyes, and once more, Berra's feathers and the Princess's eyes momentarily assumed that same turquoise glow.

Chuck's mouth fell open as he looked from Berra to the Princess and back again. "What in the world was that? I can't believe what I just saw."

Kehi explained, "It just happened on the way up here. I was pretty sure you have never seen Berra's feathers glow like that."

"I don't know what to say. What does that mean exactly?" Chuck pondered.

"We have no idea either," Sasha remarked before noticing that Salair was again blinking rapidly as if to force herself into the present.

"Princess?"

"Yes?"

"You went into a trance again. Did you see anything else?"

"Just that turquoise flower again."

"What's this?" Chuck asked, curious.

“Salair seems to fall into some sort of a trance when she looks at Berra. She saw a turquoise flower the first time her and Berra’s eyes met.”

“And it happened again just now,” the Princess confirmed.

“Sounds like it might be a key to something!” Chuck appeared lost in thought for a moment.

“That would make sense. A key to something, but to what?” Salair asked.

Then, it dawned on him as he looked over at Salair.

“What is it, Chuck?”

“Think about it, Salair, your eyes, Berra’s feathers, and your visions.”

“Yes,” she said while staring at Chuck. Then, a light went on in her head as she whispered, “Turquoise.”

“Exactly, Salair, turquoise. It must be a link to something. I guess we have another mystery to solve with Berra. She seems to be surrounded by them. I am sure Kehi told you I found her half-dead and trapped in a spider web. There is a lot of mystery surrounding her, but this turquoise incident is interesting. It might be another clue to her history. Anyway, I’m sorry, let’s talk about this note you handed Kehi. It isn’t very specific, but has something happened to your father?”

“Why yes. How did you know?”

Chuck released a prolonged sigh. “Our fathers were great friends. Our families were close, so we spent a lot of time together. When my father was killed in battle, your father made sure I was taken care of. I spent a lot of time with him at your castle after that. If you are here carrying this note, something has happened.”

Salair was thinking deeply about this information – her gaze fixated on Chuck as she tried to jog her memory. "I remember you now. You were always at the stable and armory by my father's side."

"Why yes, Salair, I can't believe you remembered that. You were pretty young at the time."

"My father was very fond of you." It went without saying that Salair always had eyes for that young man. She would watch him whenever he came over. "So, he's the one," she thought to herself.

"Thank you for saying that. I truly admire your father. He is a great man." The two just stared at each other for a second.

"I am afraid you are correct, Sir Charles," interrupted Sasha. We are here because not only has the King disappeared, but so has the Queen.

Chuck and Kehi exchanged glances before Chuck continued, "Call me Chuck, Colonel, and I am aware that, like myself, they have many enemies."

Sasha and Salair both nodded in unison as she commented, "You have done well to hide yourself."

"Considering my background, I decided I had to," Chuck replied. "How is it possible that your parents are missing? The castle is highly guarded."

Sasha glanced at Salair, who nodded for him to answer. "To be honest, Chuck, we have no idea. No one saw anything, which is alarming in itself. I can only surmise that the King's biggest enemy, the Dark Prince Drouck Helve, was the culprit. I know Drouck went back to The Dark Forest to hide for a while, but I think his hiding is over. Our sources report that he is rebuilding his army. For a while, we thought, or maybe we just hoped, he had been killed along with his father. But obviously, he wasn't."

Kehi's head jerked up. "His father, King Helve, is dead? How?"

"Yes, there was fighting amongst the heads of the different factions around the forests. Someone got to the King. I think that is part of the reason he went into hiding. In fact, my sources are convinced his son, Drouck, may have done it himself or had his great friend, Octimus, do it. Drouck hated his father."

"Whoa," said Chuck.

"Yes," asserted Sasha, "My sources also told me that Drouck stirred up a lot of trouble with the other leaders in various parts of the forest and claimed it was his father's doing. That way, he could blame any of the factions for killing his father, and no one would be the wiser. I am afraid the hiding is over, and the resurgence of his revenge against the Pishtar family is now. We suspect he is holding the King and Queen hostage and will only exchange them for the Princess."

"You know this for a fact?" asked a skeptical Kehi.

"Just a guess. The Dark Prince needs a bride to carry on his line, and it's no secret that Salair is the first one on his list. Clearly, that will never happen since I and one other guard take turns protecting the Princess; it would be impossible to kidnap her. However, I do find it quite odd that both the King and the Queen are missing."

"So do I," replied Chuck. "With all the guards on the grounds, it does seem almost impossible, Sasha."

"I don't know how to explain it otherwise. They wouldn't disappear and not tell anyone, so that just set off alarm bells for me."

"The only way they would both be missing would be if something important was going on that they couldn't talk about."

"Like what, Salair? I'm the head of security; surely, they would've told me. This is highly unusual."

"I have no idea, Sasha. That's the only thing I can think of. As long as I am safe, which I am, maybe they had to do something they couldn't tell you or anyone else."

"Well, we have to start somewhere, which is why we came to you, Chuck. I realize we are asking a lot from you and would certainly understand if you could or would not want to help us."

"Nothing you ask is too big as far as I'm concerned. After everything King Sargon has done for me and my family, I will do everything in my power to find them. Where to search is the next question."

"It is suspected that Drouck went back to The Dark Forest. You probably know that The Dark Forest is really dangerous, and whoever goes in there never comes out," said Sasha.

"I'll have my men put out some feelers. They have sources everywhere," said Chuck, glancing over at Kehi.

"I'll get on it," said Kehi.

Kehi returned after speaking with Chuck's men. "Your men are contacting their sources as we speak, Chuck."

"Good. Oshi, this is an omen. We knew if we went into hiding, bad things would start happening." Turning to his guests, he continued, "Princess and Colonel, we are ready to help in whatever way we can. I know I speak for my friend here." Glancing at Oshiro, he received an affirmative nod from his Japanese companion. "As I said, we will not sit quietly and do nothing."

"Spoken by a true warrior and friend of the King," Sasha responded.

"Thank you, Chuck," Salair said gratefully.

"If need be, we can use my fortress as our headquarters. Let's just take it one step at a time, however."

As Kehi freshened their drinks, he said, "Sir, some unwanted movement has been detected outside... something we have not seen in quite some time."

Raising his eyebrow, Chuck responded, "Oshi, I am sure you will handle any problems."

"Looking forward to it," smirked the Warrior.

"We can ill afford anyone discovering us, especially with the Princess in it."

"It appears our solitude has come to an end, Oshi."

"Well, sir, it has been a little too quiet around here."

"We knew this day would come. In fact, I think we were hoping for it."

"We may have been gone for too long from the sounds of things."

"I agree. Bad things are starting to spike up again, and this time, we must put an end to all of it."

"Agreed," nodded Kehi, looking very stern.

Kehi, on the other hand, was born in the Orient and was masterfully trained in the art of Imperial Combat. His fighting skills have never been seen in this part of the world.

The Princess asked, "Is anything wrong?"

"Nothing that we cannot handle for the moment," Chuck assured her.

"We were so very careful," Sasha worried. "I hope we have not given away your whereabouts."

"Nothing we can't handle," Chuck repeated, "Believe me."

"When Chuck says, 'believe me', he means it," Kehi rarely missed an opportunity to brag about his friend. "I am not sure you are aware Princess, but his mastery of weapons is world-class. Chuck's father was a great warrior. Chuck's great-grandfather handed down his mastery of weapons to his son and Chuck's father to him. They were taught about every weapon they could get their hands on and spent hours and hours a day mastering various deadly weapons."

"Impressive," commented the Princess.

Kehi excused himself while Sir Charles and his guests continued conversing. He abruptly returned and nodded mysteriously to Chuck.

Sir Charles turned to his visitors, "I'm sure you are very weary from traveling. Kehi, would you be kind enough to show our guests to the lower section and see if they have everything they might need."

Sasha realized they were being politely dismissed.

"Yes, I am actually quite tired. Thank you for everything," said Salair.

"Of course, Your Highness," said Chuck, bowing.

"Sasha, when you are ready, I believe you are needed back upstairs. I will make sure one of the guards shows you the way while another guard will stay with the Princess."

"I'll be right up," assured Sasha.

"Please follow me," said Kehi. He led them to a small elevator and chanted something in Japanese. The door slid open, and he motioned for them to enter.

As they glided downward, Sasha remarked, "This is truly clever."

"Yes, it has come in handy once or twice, but we haven't had an occasion lately to use it," explained Kehi. Sir Charles had it built as another layer of security."

The floor stopped, the door opened, and they were led to another dead end. "What in the world?" whispered Salair softly to Sasha, who silently shook his head. Before them stood an ancient, giant, petrified tree trunk. Then again, Kehi whispered something, and in the blink of an eye, an opening appeared.

"Please come in," said Kehi casually, as if such things happened every day.

Salair could no longer contain herself. "This is the most unusual and amazing place I have ever seen!"

Sasha agreed. "Yes, it's quite extraordinary, although I am going to have to brush up on my Japanese."

"Indeed, you will," laughed Kehi before becoming more sedate.

"It is definitely safe down here," he assured them. Opening the door to a beautifully furnished suite, "Here you are Princess." Salair raised her eyebrows in delightful surprise at the comforts the room exhibited. Their host then stepped across the hall to another door, which revealed a room with the same comforts. "Sasha, you will be right here. If either of you needs anything, let the guards know. Please make yourselves comfortable. We will dine upstairs in about an hour. I trust that will give you a little time to rest and freshen up if that is okay with you, Your Highness?"

"It does indeed, and thank you for everything, Kehi."

"Certainly, Princess. Colonel, when you are ready, come upstairs. A guard will guide you the way, and another one will remain close by the Princess."

"I'll be right up," said Sasha as he entered his chambers. Kehi hurried to confer with Chuck's men guarding the compound.

Upstairs, Sir Charles was conversing with his guards about securing the castle prior to embarking on their unexpected but greatly anticipated quest. He turned as Kehi entered, "Ah, Kehi. What exactly is going on outside?"

"I am not entirely sure, sir, but our guards have slain five very weird creatures snooping around the grounds."

"What do you mean, weird creatures?" Chuck asked.

"They looked to be half man, half rat," replied a very puzzled Kehi. "Never seen anything like that before."

"That is weird," agreed the Nobleman thoughtfully, "From a different forest, I would assume?" As careful as Sasha and the Princess were, they were obviously followed. "Everyone is to be on watch tonight, and no one suspicious is to be spared. Understood?"

"Yes, Sir Charles understood," his men replied in unison.

Chuck and Kehi went inside to meet with Sasha before the Princess returned for dinner. The moment Sasha entered the room, Chuck asked him the question on everyone's mind.

"Do you have any idea where Drouck took Salair's parents? I can only guess they have been taken to Drouck's castle in The Dark Forest."

"But that wouldn't make any sense," said Kehi.

"It would be too obvious," countered Sasha.

“Exactly,” said Kehi.

“But in any case, we don’t even know where the castle is,” said Sasha.

A guard burst into the room, “Excuse me, sir, but we have captured someone snooping around. He has screamed something interesting.”

“We thought he might have the information we could use,” added Chuck’s head of security, Benjamin, who entered and spoke in a more restrained and dignified manner.

“Well done, Benjamin,” Chuck nodded his approval. “Escort him to the ‘office’.”

“At once, sir.”

“Let’s see who this character is,” said Chuck.

“Kehi, you know what equipment we’ll need.”

“Indeed, I do,” he said and left the room.

Chuck switched his attention to Sasha. “I trust you’ll join us? The Princess is safe and has a guard outside her room.”

“I would indeed.”

They met Benjamin outside ‘the office’. It was a large, dark room mostly used for storage but also an excellent place for interrogation. Benjamin opened the door for them. “Well, well, look what came out of the rat hole,” exclaimed Chuck, staring at a very ugly rat with only one functioning eye and a shredded ear. The rat was deposited in the center of the room and bound tightly enough to make breathing possible but difficult.

Chuck continued speaking while circling the captive, “Well if it isn’t my old friend! What are you doing snooping around here, Shift? I thought the beating you took last time would have been enough for you. You must not have known I was here."

"I knew you were here," snarled Shift.

"No one knows I'm here. You were just dumb enough to get caught."

In irritation, Sir Charles drew his sword and pressed the sharply honed point against his prisoner's neck, drawing a trickle of blood. "Why are you snooping around here?"

"I need your help," gagged the squirming rat.

Chuck stepped back. "Still a liar! Have you learned nothing, Shift? You hate me, and I hate you. Let's try it again. Why are you here?"

Sasha stood off in the darkness and watched with mounting interest.

"Kehi, if you will please," directed Sir Charles.

Kehi stepped forward with 'the equipment', which consisted of a small jar containing three tiny red spiders.

"As you please," smiled Chuck, motioning toward the jar.

"No!" cried the terrified Shift. "I am telling you the truth! I swear... I need your help! Drouck has gone off the deep end. He's even more of a schizophrenic than he ever was. He is building a new powerful army of manras."

"Manras?" Repeated Sir Charles with a bewildered glance at Shift. "What is a manra? And what else? You wouldn't be looking for me unless there were something else... something extremely important, or you would not have jeopardized yourself by coming here."

Shift spoke rapidly and shakily, "He was ranting about King Pishtar, about how the King had stolen what was rightfully his throne and that the Kingdom is rightfully his. He mentioned something about getting hold of the Princess and making the King's family pay for what they had done to him."

Taking the jar of deadly spiders from Kehi's hand, Chuck pressed it against the trembling rat's forehead, "You don't care one little bit about the Princess or her family. Now, tell me the truth! And for the second time, what is a manra?"

Shift just stared at the jar of spiders; he seemed paralyzed to speak.

"All right, I have had enough of this." Chuck returned the jar to Kehi with one simple word, "Please."

"Wait, wait! I have a daughter... I have a daughter! I need your help!" he cried as he slumped forward and fainted.

CHAPTER 2

"Great," muttered Chuck, looking down at Shift. "He has a daughter? That's hard to believe, but what would that have to do with anything? Oshi, have the men carry him in the back and let him rest. He looks like hell. Nothing new, of course. Make sure he is tied up. I don't want him loose by any means. I still don't believe him. There's something weird going on."

"At once, Chuck," Kehi replied.

Chuck turned to Sasha and said, "Let's go back inside and get some dinner. I'll deal with Shift later."

"I'm assuming you know this character," Sasha said with a deep chuckle.

"Yes, we go way back. I cannot believe he was stupid enough to try to find me," Chuck replied, "but this may work in our favor after all."

"Maybe he is telling the truth," suggested Sasha.

"I don't know, I just don't know. He has always been a seedy, lying character. I can't imagine he would even have a daughter," Chuck responded.

The Princess appeared at the door with wide-open eyes, "What's happening?" Chuck relayed to her the preceding incident. "Wow!" was her only comment.

"What are you going to do with this Shift character?" Sasha probed.

"I don't know yet. I need to think about it."

Chuck was spared the mental exercise when he noticed the chef standing in the doorway. "Excuse me sir, dinner is ready, if you please."

"Yes, thank you Maurice. I am certain our guests are famished." Chuck then addressed Kehi, "Is our other guest secure?"

"Yes, pretty secure. He won't be going anywhere."

"Excellent. Well then, let's see what Maurice has prepared for us."

Dinner was divine, even by royal standards.

"I am going to have to steal your chef once this is all over," exclaimed the Princess.

"He may want to go with you once this is over," laughed Chuck, laying aside his plate. "Amusing story there. He was one of our carpenters when we first started building this place. Every now and then, Maurice would disappear into the kitchen and return with the most delicious meal for the crew. It was obvious he was quite gifted in the kitchen, so I hired him away from my foreman, and the rest is history."

After the laughter subsided, Sasha brought them back into the moment, "Sir Charles, with everything that is happening, I must apologize. It appears we have brought danger to your door."

"Don't worry, Sasha, you risked your lives getting here." Pushing aside his concern, "We are all safe here. My men are highly trained. Nothing gets by them."

The following morning, Sir Charles, Kehi, and Sasha returned to confront a sleeping Shift. "Wake up!" yelled Chuck as he sharply slapped Shift across his big snout.

The slap stunned Shift awake. "Hey! What's going on?"

Chuck immediately began interrogating him, "You say you have a daughter? I don't believe you."

"I don't care if you believe me, but it's true. Drouck killed my wife and took my daughter." Tears appeared on his anguished face.

Chuck looked at Kehi in utter astonishment. He had never seen Shift like this.

Kehi repeated softly, "Drouck killed your wife?"

"Yes."

"Explain yourself, now."

"I was at his forecastle doing my patrol," Shift started. "Obviously, because I wasn't home, Drouck took a couple of his manras went to my house and took my daughter, Nia. When my wife tried to stop them, he stabbed her."

"How do you know this?" Kehi persisted.

"That night, when I went home, my wife lay there bleeding, but my daughter was nowhere to be found. My wife barely lived long enough to tell me what happened. I raced to the castle to confront

Drouck. My daughter was there all right. He was holding a dagger to her throat and told me to get out. He said he would kill her if he ever saw my face again. His guards, who I thought were my friends, beat me up and threw me out."

"I don't know if I can believe you," murmured an unsure Sir Charles. "You could be making up this whole story just because we've captured you."

"I swear it's true!" wailed a distraught Shift. "I just want to get my daughter away from him. He's crazy, and I don't know what kind of harm will come to her. Please help me. I am not lying," he said, fighting back his tears.

"Tell me about the manras. Who or what are they?" demanded Chuck.

Shift readily complied. "Prince Drouck has this large room in his forecastle that is kept locked. When new recruits arrive, he sends them into that room on their first night. When they leave the next morning, they start changing. Their eyes have a slight red glow to them, they develop fangs and their nails turn into claws. They are angry, aggressive, and carry out whatever orders Drouck gives them."

"What causes that transformation?" Chuck probed for more information.

"I don't know exactly, but I have heard rumors that some sort of mysterious gas is piped into the room while they are sleeping."

"What kind of gas?" asked Chuck.

"I have no clue. Nobody seems to know, but if a soldier refuses to go in the room, they are never seen again."

Sir Charles was silent for a few moments, pondering the information he had received thus far. Then he continued, "What and where is this forecastle?" Chuck inquired.

"His main castle is somewhere in the darkest part of The Dark Forest. No one dares to go that far, so the location of his main castle remains a mystery. The forecastle we guard is in a less remote part of the forest. He warehouses supplies and weapons at this location. Like I said, it also serves as a training place for his army."

Sir Charles studied Shift intently for several seconds before saying, "We'll be back." Chuck and Kehi went outside.

"That is very interesting information, Oshi," Chuck began.

"Agreed. But the prospects of finding the King and Queen at that location doesn't sound very promising."

"Yes, but if he is telling the truth, locating one of his castles would be a major accomplishment. No one has been able to find him or his castles in a very long time."

"The downside to that is we don't know how many manras are at the training facility. It could be extremely risky to simply walk in there with Shift. What if it is a trap?"

"I think we need another round of our little spider friends to see if he is actually telling the truth," decided Chuck. "We'll come back later. We'll need a layout of this forecastle and more information about the number of manras we may face."

"I totally agree."

"Ask the guards to check the perimeter again and wait a few hours just to make sure he didn't bring any other manras, as he calls them, with him."

"I'm on it," said Kehi. "I don't think the initial five manras we killed were with Shift, and we haven't seen any other activity so far, but I'll I talk to the men and have them make a thorough search. I'll see you inside."

As Kehi departed to complete his tasks, Chuck summoned his chief guard, Benjamin. "See that Shift gets a little food and water. Don't let him out of your sight."

Chuck went back inside and continued conversing with Salair and Sasha, concluding with, "I don't completely believe his story, but the good thing is, he is now captive, and we can use him to get to Drouck's castle."

"I can't believe it. His poor wife and daughter," said Salair sympathetically.

Chuck maintained his distrust of the entire situation. "I still don't completely believe his story. But if he is telling the truth, we have lucked out for sure. If he leads us to one of Drouck's castles, it will benefit all of us."

At that moment, Kehi entered the room. "Excuse me sir, the grounds are secure. The men have seen nothing out there."

"Thank you, Oshi. Maybe the old rat is telling the truth after all." Sir Charles seemed to relax a bit. "Come join us. Since we have a new tag-a-long, we must keep your hair under wraps, Princess."

"So, you know?"

"Yes."

"Know what?" asked a confused Kehi.

Sasha answered for Sir Charles, "The black tips at the end of Salair's hair are inherent in the bloodline of the Pishtar Family, specifically on her mother's side."

"I am not sure our intruder would know that, but we cannot afford to take that risk," Chuck informed them.

"We cannot," said Sasha. "It makes me very nervous having Shift around the Princess, even though I'm sure he will have no idea who she is."

"I know," nodded Chuck, "but all precautions will be taken."

"I don't mind a bit," asserted the Princess forcefully. "We made it this far and will continue to do whatever is necessary. I will not stop until I find my parents."

"Hopefully, Shift will have a direct but less dangerous route for us," Kehi added.

"Well, he made it this far, so that says something, I suppose," Sasha murmured doubtfully.

"I can't believe what I just heard from Shift. Manras don't sound good, but at least we can spot them a lot easier now. The red glow in their eyes is definitely a dead giveaway." Chuck exclaimed, "We will need to get word to other parts of the forest about this."

Kehi nodded his head in total agreement and said, "Most definitely, since it sounds like Drouck is trying to rebuild his army to match what his father used to have."

"Except they are not the caliber of soldiers his father had. He will have to be stopped at all costs. And I, by the way, am somewhat familiar with The Dark Forest and will know if Shift is leading us astray," Sasha stated.

They all stared at him. "How can you know anything about The Dark Forest?" Kehi asked.

"That is one area that everyone in the land is afraid of, and yet you've made it in and out safely?"

Sasha sighed miserably and put his head down for a few seconds before answering the question. "It was a long time ago and one of the most frightening and horrible experiences of my entire life."

He then began telling his story.

CHAPTER 3

"My grandfather was a general at the start of King Helve's new reign. At that time, armies were ruled by kings and handed down to their heirs, just as royal titles were," started Sasha. "King Helve's father's army was the single most powerful army in the world back then. Not only was it respected by all, but it was also highly feared. However, things started to change when King Helve's father handed his army down to his son. King Helve II was nothing like his father. He was five years old when his mother, the Queen, died from cancer. The King didn't have much time to spend with him, and unfortunately, he fell under the influence of evil and designing conspirators who succeeded beyond their wildest dreams. As a young adult, the Prince had become adept at scheming, manipulating, and hiding his true feelings from his father. The unsuspecting King trusted him completely, and on the Prince's thirtieth birthday, he even gifted the deceitful Prince control of the army. It was then that the delighted and devious Prince began transforming it to fit his own malicious purposes. He recruited soldiers that were nothing more than murderers and thieves. They had no respect for anyone outside their reformed military model. Slowly but surely, the army changed in such an evil direction that all the effective and patriotic soldiers were forced out by the new corrupt order. When his father, King Helve I, finally realized what was happening, it was already too late. He had no choice but to flee back to the Valley of the Caverns."

Sasha continued, "King Helve II was the epitome of ruthlessness and evil. After the birth of his son, now Prince Drouck, he banished the Queen from the kingdom, threatening to take her life if she were ever to return. He raised his son by himself, teaching him the ways of torture and cruelty. Without a mother or any form of kindness, Prince Drouck became as psychotic as his father, or perhaps, many said, even worse.

"On his eighteenth birthday, King Helve II put Prince Drouck in charge of his army. After that, both the King and the Prince became even more draconian. Everything started drastically changing. My father, realizing the terrible consequences of these changes, tried to discuss them with King Helve II. When Prince Drouck found this out, it angered him so much that he had my dad savagely beaten. He ordered my dad to leave and never return, or his entire family would be killed. The King stood by and said nothing. My dad was horrified and dismayed to see the King and the Prince destroy what was once a highly respected army.

"When he got home that night, he opened the door and fell into the house. He was so severely wounded; I don't even know how he even made it home. My mother and I bandaged him up as best we could. He related his confrontation with the Prince and the subsequent events to us. He said he didn't trust the Prince or his father and was afraid they would show up at our cottage any minute. Despite our strong objection, he insisted we quickly pack a few necessities and leave our house that very night. In an attempt to keep our departure inconspicuous, I accompanied my mother in one direction while my father went another. We planned to meet at a specific time and place the next morning. My father never arrived at our meeting place."

Sadness flickered in his eyes as he went on. "Disregarding my mother's protests, I forced her to hide in one of the numerous but secret caves my friends and I had discovered and played in when we were kids. I set out to find my father. For several hours, I searched the forest. Not wanting to leave my mother alone for too long, I started to turn back when I suddenly spied the Prince with a small army just ahead of me. I hurriedly climbed a tree so I could observe them without being seen.

"I saw that my father was with them. He and the Prince were face to face, shouting at each other. My dad was being held back by Drouck's men. Drouck began walking away from my dad when he abruptly whirled around, drew his sword, and stabbed my father in the chest, killing him instantly. I was horrified and let out a huge cry. I couldn't help it. Of course, Drouck saw me and commanded his men to kill me too.

"At that moment, all I could think about was my mother. I could not get killed, for she would never know what happened. I leaped from the tree and ran as fast as I could back to the cave where my mother hid, and then we waited. Drouck's army searched for me to no avail. We waited another day before returning to bury my father. It was the worst thing I ever went through. My mother never recovered from her grief, and just a few months later, she died."

Everyone in the room was completely silent.

"Colonel," said Chuck, "You do not need to go any further. I can see this is very painful for you."

"I'm okay," Sasha lifted his head up. "It's nice to get this off my chest. I have never told anyone before."

Chuck nodded.

"After we buried my dad, my mother and I fled into the wilderness, living in caves, fighting darkness and dodging savages and nasty creatures. I knew Drouck would never give up looking for me. Both of us were very weak. Food and water were scarce. I think we were delirious at one point and became totally lost. All I remember is that we stumbled and fell into this weird pile of leaves, and the next thing we knew, we were face to face with the most peculiar animal – a fuzzar. Knowing what I know now about fuzzars, my mom and I were most fortunate he didn't kill us then and there. I can only conclude that he felt sorry for us. A boy and his mother, half-starved and totally lost, stumbling onto his property. He took us into his house, fed us, and let us recuperate.

"To this day, I am very grateful for my old friend Keewae. He knew about The Dark Forest; in fact, there was another forest, The Magic Forest, that we had never heard of. Keewae lives on the outer perimeter of it. Very smart on his part as it serves as a partial protective barrier from the dark forces. The Magic Forest, although beautiful, is deceptively dangerous and deadly."

"Your friend, Keewae, sounds amazing and dangerous at the same time," interrupted Kehi.

"Let's just say I am glad he befriended us" concluded Sasha.

"What does a fuzzar look like?" asked the Princess.

Sasha began his description of a fuzzar. "A fuzzar looks like a black bear but walks on two legs. Also, the fur on the top of his head is about four inches longer than the rest of his body. It is not actually fur, but sensitive tentacles that detect danger... it is sort of a unique alarm system, if you will. This allows the fuzzar to move around the forest a bit easier with its danger detector. Fuzzars also have razor-sharp claws. One of the claws on each paw can extend outward about a foot and is used for stabbing food or slashing its enemies. They are also perfect for piercing the hard shells of beetles which roam The Magic Forest."

"You mean, like a knife blade?" asked the Princess.

"Precisely, my dear."

"Interesting," she mused.

Continuing his narrative, Sasha said, "Fuzzars are very intelligent and untrusting by nature. They eat various vegetables, nuts, and especially beetles. Their favorite things in the whole world to eat are the swirly, fuzzy caterpillar and the hourglass beetle. Wouldn't you know it? The Magic Forest is one of the places you can find hourglass beetles and swirly caterpillars. The hourglass beetles also serve as the Queen's spies."

"What Queen?" interrupted Princess Salair.

"Queen Morphina," replied Sasha. "She is a bitter, cruel, and evil butterfly. Unlike regular butterflies with beautiful patterns and colors, Morphina had an oddly shaped body with splotchy coloring. The only redeeming color on her was a small patch of brilliant turquoise right between her strangely shaped wings. Word is, something happened to her cocoon, causing her deformity. Because of that, she hides in a dark castle ruled by Coridon."

"Coridon?" asked Kehi.

"Yes. Coridon, a crusty, crab-like beetle creature, who controls her beetles through telepathy. She is the overlord of the beetle world and associates herself with The Dark Forest and Prince Drouck. No one knows exactly where her castle is. It is rumored that her hourglass beetles are scattered all over the area, leading up to her castle. She sees anyone in her area through them. If they are unfriendly, they are met with an unkindly death. They align themselves with all kinds of nasty leaders, the octospy being one of them. It's half tarantula, half octopus. Very, very nasty indeed. Rumor has it, Coridon has helped turn a lot of forests dark, including one of the most special forests, The Valley of the Waterfalls and Flowers. Very, very sad."

Berra was in the room listening. When she heard Sasha mention The Valley of the Waterfalls and Flowers, her turquoise feathers once again took on a glow as she flapped her wings and sang a happy melody.

"Whoa!" exclaimed Chuck. "That's never been sung before."

"I have never heard that either, and her feathers are glowing again," added Kehi.

"Incredible," continued Chuck. "Berra, do you know The Valley of the Waterfalls and Flowers?" With feathers glowing again, Berra flapped her wings and sang the same sound again.

"Very perplexing," observed Chuck.

"Sounds like another clue for us to piece together about her," Kehi replied. "I am sorry," apologized Kehi, "go ahead, Sasha."

Sasha went on to say, "Fortunately for us, Keewae despises Prince Drouck. So, once we felt better, he helped us get through the forest unharmed. We probably would have perished if it were not for him."

"What an incredible story!" Sir Charles remarked.

"I feel bad, Sasha. I never knew that about your family. I'm sorry you had to endure something so awful," said the Princess.

"Thank you, Princess. It's not something that was ever easy to talk about, but it was good to get it off my chest."

"Well, it sounds like Keewae is a good ally to have," she said cheerily.

"No doubt, Salair, no doubt."

"Well," said Chuck, "we have a daunting task ahead of us." Chuck concluded, "In light of Shift's appearance, we would need an extra horse to tie him to. I'm taking no chances with that weasel. Princess and Sasha, if I may, you should try to get as much rest today since we will leave tonight in the darkness."

"Sasha and I are more than able to help you get ready," offered the Princess.

"Thank you, Princess," smiled Sir Charles. "If you would just make sure you have everything you need, my men will do the rest. Just let me know if you need anything else."

"Yes, of course," replied Salair and Sasha in unison.

"If you will excuse us, we have some arrangements to make," Chuck told them. Turning to Kehi, "See that the horses are ready to go this evening. We'll need full gear for them as well."

"Most certainly, Chuck."

"Thank you for everything," gushed the Princess. "I don't know what we would have done if we had not found you. Your generosity is above anything we could have expected."

"Yes," Sasha hurried to agree. "Your service to the kingdom remains unflappable."

"It is my honor," replied an embarrassed Sir Charles, who was not accustomed to receiving compliments this effusively, especially by a Princess. He was trying to back out of the room as gracefully as possible before they could see that he was blushing furiously. "Be well!"

"Kehi, I'll go talk to our other guest," said Chuck, winking at him.

“Shift, I have some news for you!” Sir Charles told his prisoner. “We’ll help you get your daughter back. You will be tied to one of my horses the whole way. I don’t trust you at all.”

“Tied up?” repeated an indignant Shift.

“Yep,” he replied. “If you don’t like that, the other option is our spider friends. Take it or leave it.”

“I’ll take it,” Shift replied through gritted teeth, as he feared the deadly spiders above all else.

“I thought you would. We leave tonight.”

CHAPTER 4

Kehi, followed by several guards, headed to the stables to prepare the horses for their upcoming journey. Oshiro Kehi, named after his great-grandfather, was a proud descendant of one of the few royal Samurai families hailing from Japan. He was never without the sword his great-grandfather handed down to him. Inscribed on the blade was a mysterious symbol and their family crest. Like all his family, he was raised and led his life according to the ethic code of bushido, which is "the way of the warrior," self-disciplined, respectful, and ethical behavior.

Chuck returned to the house to pack his armor, swords, and other weapons. After all, he was expecting some very unpleasant confrontations. He then went to meet Kehi at the stables to ensure everything was in order with his prized Arabian horses.

Chuck's great-grandmother had gifted him an unusual bloodline of Arabian horses. These animals sprang from Al Khamsat al Raul, the five great breeds of Arabian horses. His current steeds were very important to him. Throughout the generations, this singular breed of Arabian horses had been bred by his great-grandmother's ancestors. She wanted to ensure that her descendants would be well-mounted and protected in battle. And indeed, Chuck's Arabian steeds had saved his life on more than one occasion. This ancient breed's enhancements, albeit by his great-grandmother, resulted in razor-sharp hooves and keen hearing that detected any sound within a half mile. Not only that, their extra-perceptive night vision and speed, exceeding that of a cheetah, were unparalleled compared to other creatures.

The saddles Chuck used were as unique as the mounts they adorned. Constructed of exceedingly thick, strong, and durable rhinoceros hide, the saddles had special slits in the leather that could easily accommodate swords, axes, crossbows, and other such weapons as the rider deemed necessary.

Chuck approached his horses almost reverently and gently stroked one smooth nose after another, murmuring, "My beauties." They shook their heads and neighed softly in greeting.

"I am here to ask you to make a long and dangerous journey one more time," said Chuck. The beautiful animals continued shaking their heads up and down, waving their silky manes and whinnying as if they understood every word he was uttering. He began saddling the horses once Kehi came out with the supplies while Sasha tagged along behind him.

"Good evening, Chuck," said Sasha. "The Princess is on her way."

"Very good," replied Chuck.

"Where is Shift?" inquired Sasha, looking around.

"He'll be the last one to come up. We have decided to tie him to a horse. We can't take any risks!"

The Princess appeared wearing simple clothing with a grey hooded cloak. She made sure to tie her hair up to avoid exposing the black tips. Nevertheless, she was still beautiful, and Chuck, somewhat distracted by her appearance, took a moment to admire her.

"Good evening, Your Highness."

"Good evening, Chuck. I insist you call me Salair."

"As you wish, Salair," he said as he continued to admire her beauty and elegance.

Sasha approached the horses. "Wow Chuck, you said we would be riding ponies. But...these are the most beautiful stallions I have ever seen!" He exclaimed, studying the unusual animals with an appreciative eye.

"Thank you, Sasha," answered Chuck. "Let me introduce both of you to my precious stallions. This is Sleet," Chuck said, resting his hand on the neck of a sparking, pure-white animal. "And this is his twin brother, Tarr, black as midnight!" Indeed, the alert stallion did not have a speck of white anywhere on him. "This one here is Mirka," introduced Chuck while rubbing his nose. It was of a boiling shimmering caramel candy color with a coal-black mane and tail. "Next is Willow, Mirka's cousin." Even in the dim stable, Willow's golden body and white mane were glistening. Finally, Chuck arrived proudly at the last horse. "And this one is Shia." Sasha looked appreciatively at the fiery red mount, whose broad, muscled chest appeared to be the largest of the five stallions. Shia was of the Icelandic breed of horses with a lineage dating back 10,000 years. The other four beauties descended from the Caspian Horse breed that dated back to 3000 B.C.

"Very impressive indeed," said the Princess as she stepped forward to stroke each horse.

After the introduction, Chuck went on to give instructions. "Salair, you will ride Willow. Sasha, you ride Mirka. Kehi will take Tarr.

We will tie our prisoner on Shia. I usually ride Sleet. Berra, my girl, you keep a watch out for us." Berra nodded and whistled, understanding every word.

They were all wearing tattered clothing and looked like a disheveled bunch. Then, turning toward the Princess, Chuck said, "Since I am not sure if Shift is familiar with you or your family name, let's call you 'Ally' if you don't mind. And for now, you will be my cousin."

"Of course... Cousin," smirked Salair, but she appreciated his concern for her safety.

"I think that is wise," agreed Sasha. "We must protect her from anyone and everyone."

"Benjamin," Chuck called, "bring up Shift, but be sure that he is blindfolded at all times."

Benjamin went to the 'office', blindfolded Shift, and said, "Let's go."

They brought him out and threw him up on Shia.

"Tie his legs to the stirrups and his hands to the saddle horn," instructed Chuck.

"This is unnecessary," protested Shift.

"Quiet," commanded Chuck, "or I'll happily gag you. We will not take any chances."

Then he turned to Benjamin and whispered, "Have a few men follow us for a few miles, just in case. Make sure they stay hidden."

"You got it, sir," replied Benjamin.

CHAPTER 5

"Why are you back here?" cried Prince Drouck to his unwelcome Captain Smack.

"I need more manras," Smack answered. "We are missing five of our men."

"What do you mean, missing five men?" yelled the irate Prince. "What happened to them?"

"I don't know. We were in an area where we thought we saw the Princess, and in a blink of an eye, both she and our manras were nowhere to be found. As if they disappeared in thin air," explained the leery officer.

"First, you almost let the Queen escape, and now you have lost track of the Princess!" Prince Drouck's eyes were turning a deeper red due to his extreme anger. "Take more manras, as many as you want, and find them!" screamed Drouck. Grabbing Smack by the neck, Prince Drouck said in a low yet threatening voice, "Don't you dare come back without her."

"Yes, sir," Smack answered in a strangled voice.

Drouck shoved Smack backward and reiterated, “Don’t come back without her! Understood?”

“Yes, Prince,” answered Smack as he backed carefully and thankfully out of the room. He knew full well that Drouck’s deep red eyes were a warning to him. The Prince was about to have one of his episodes of rage—the kind of rage you would never want to be around.

Smack was becoming increasingly disgusted by Drouck and his vile nature. He was growing weary of watching him destroy what used to be an admirable and formidable army. Sadly, Smack dared not say that to anyone, knowing he would be killed instantly. He was well aware that Drouck was nothing more than a madman and decided to take more manras, point them in the right direction, and save himself.

“Let’s start here and fan out in that direction,” Smack said unwittingly, pointing in the exact direction the Princess was now traveling.

“Yes, sir,” answered all the manras obediently as they spread out to begin their search.

Captain Smack watched them disperse in the darkness and waited till they disappeared. He snuck back to the forecastle, packed up his things, and faded into the darkness, never to return.

After Smack left, Prince Drouck went into a wild rage, and unable to control his anger, he started trashing the room he was in. This wasn’t the first time his uncontrollable temper had led to destructive outbursts. Even when he was younger, his fits of rage would result in his father locking him in a room until he calmed down. He has been blinded by that rage ever since. He was pacing furiously back and forth, muttering madly, “The Princess must be found. Let’s see what I can get out of her mother.” He screamed, “Nia… Nia!”

"Yes, Drouck," Nia cowered in, noticing the red eyes and trashed room.

"Is that woman awake yet?"

"No, she wasn't the last time I checked on her." Nia lied because she knew Drouck would hit her again, and she just couldn't stand to watch it.

Drouck just stared straight through Nia. "Keep me advised. Let me know when she comes to. I'll be back in an hour. Get this room cleaned up."

"Of course, Your Highness."

"The House of Darkwick will reign again, Nia. Now get out!"

Breathing a sigh of relief, Nia happily backed out and went to check on the prisoner.

CHAPTER 6

The group began its journey, and Charles placed the Princess between himself and Kehi. As Sleet was white, he had to be camouflaged as well.

Shift had told them that reaching The Dark Forest would take two full days. Once they were a safe distance away from the house, Chuck removed Shift's blindfold so he could guide the group.

"This won't be an easy route," Shift informed. "This route is very thick with shrubs and trees. We will have to ride single file for many hours. Not very easy," he grumbled.

"Are you sure this is the only way we can get to his forecastle?" asked Chuck.

"Well, if you don't want to get caught, we must go this way. It is one of the few routes Drouck's manras don't know about."

"If you know this route, why wouldn't they?" Kehi snapped.

"Because I am old, and through the years, I have learned a lot of different ways around this god-forsaken forest."

Just then, several piercing cries rang out.

"Let's get on with it then," Chuck ordered anxiously. "It sounds like we have company."

He was gravely concerned for the safety of the Princess and, thus, greatly relieved that he had told Benjamin to trail them.

"Follow me," Shift called and galloped Shia along the trail he had chosen.

They rode steadily and silently, only stopping briefly to rest and make sure they weren't being followed. It was the second day, and while the others were sleeping, Kehi stood guard with Berra perched on a branch above him. With her keen eyesight, Berra noticed something moving in the darkness and abruptly uttered a low whistle.

"What is it girl?" Kehi asked, glancing up. Kehi took a double take at Berra. Her golden feathers had turned a dark, reddish-orange hue. His mouth was agape as he lost his train of thought for a moment. Berra whistled again, interrupting his shock. "Sorry, right, Berra." Approximately two hundred yards in front of him, he observed several black figures darting from tree to tree.

"Chuck, wake up," whispered Kehi, jolting him out of his sleep.

"What is it?" asked Chuck, shaking his head to force himself to become alert.

"Berra spotted some dark figures about two hundred yards out."

"Wake up everyone," Sir Charles commanded, striding to where Shift was sleeping. He went over and gagged Shift just in case he decided to call out. "We have visitors," whispering over to Sasha and the Princess. "Sasha, stay here with Ally and keep an eye on Shift. Oshi, let's go." The two warriors took off toward the dark figures, swords in hand.

Kehi placed a cautionary hand on his friend's arm and pointed ahead. They nodded knowingly to each other and crept forward. Before you knew it, two manras were dead and drug under shrubbery, and then another.

A high, shrill whistle pierced the darkness. "Listen, Oshi," murmured Chuck, halting his movements. "Is that Tarr?"

"This way, Chuck," called out Kehi as they ran toward a snorting, whinnying black stallion. Tarr was rearing up and thrashing his razor-sharp hooves at two more manras.

"Get away from him!" shouted Chuck. The manras wheeled around just as Kehi let go of his sword, hurling it into the heart of one of the two, striking him dead. The other one came at Chuck, but not before Tarr could rear up and deliver a smashing blow to his head, killing him instantly.

"Berra," Chuck commanded, "make sure no one else is coming." Berra took off, and after a few minutes of circling the area, she flew back and landed on Chuck's raised forearm. As she landed, her feathers returned to their beautiful golden sheen, and then, she whistled a high note.

"Oshi, I don't know what to say. Am I seeing things? Did you see that? Did Berra just change colors?"

"No, you're not seeing things. I can only tell you that once she sensed we were in danger and saw those manras coming at us, her feathers turned dark, reddish-orange."

"Well, I guess since she has been safe with us all this time, there was never a need for her to be alarmed. I surmise that is why we have never seen that before. Let's get back to the others Oshi. Let's keep this to ourselves for now."

"Right Chuck, especially since Shift is around."

Chuck said as he approached Tarr, "Once again, you've placed yourself in danger to protect us. You're amazing Tarr, but you're scaring me. I guess I owe you one." Tarr nudged Chuck. "I know boy, you're the best. You too, Berra. Good teamwork!" Berra chirped.

"I hope they are all right. They have been gone too long," a worried Salair whispered to Sasha. They were well hidden with the horses. Sasha was nervously pacing the ground, looking at Shift, and staring through branches into the distance. He seemed pretty anxious as he tried to figure out what their next move would be if the two warriors didn't return.

"Ah, there they are!" He whistled softly to help them find their way to them.

"Are you guys okay? What happened?" cried Salair, the worry evident in her voice.

"Everything is fine," replied Chuck, dismounting near Shift and yanking the gag from his mouth. "There were more manras than we expected. We had to chase down Tarr, who was chasing down a manra that got by us."

"I told you Drouck would hunt us down!" snapped Shift.

"Well, it will be hard for a dead manra to do any hunting, right Shift?" retorted Kehi.

"You should be thanking us, you wretch," said Chuck, glaringly.

"Well, I say what an impressive force you all are, between Tarr and Berra and the two of you," chimed in the Princess, "the manras don't stand a chance."

"Thanks, cousin, but we had better get a move on," said Chuck, still glaring at Shift. "Get up, Shift. How much further is it?"

"We're getting close," he grumbled.

"The sooner, the better," muttered Kehi.

"It's good news and bad news," Shift warned. "This part of the forest gets thicker and darker. It will be difficult to see any distance ahead of us. We'll have to go in single file."

"My horses have excellent night vision, so following you won't be an issue. Just lead the way. Now get going," Sir Charles barked.

Shift, who was extremely agitated, opened his mouth to say something, but Kehi interrupted him, "You're in no position to say a word. So, get going!"

Chuck nodded to the large golden bird on his shoulder. "Berra, fly ahead if you would, and keep an eye out." Berra chirped once, and flapping her powerful wings, she soared upward through the darkness.

After another hour of manipulating themselves through the pitch-black and rough, rugged forest, they came to a clearing. Shift turned and whispered, "It is just up ahead."

"Everyone dismount for a second while we figure this out," instructed Sir Charles.

"How many guards does Drouck have here?" Sir Charles inquired as the golden bird dropped from the sky to land on his shoulder.

"Around twenty guards are there at any given time."

"Great," muttered Kehi. "So... Chuck, what's our plan?"

"We need to find a secure hiding place for my cousin Ally. I don't want her any closer than this."

The Princess shifted her hood back a bit, looking over at Chuck.

Sasha was looking around at the forest very intently.

"What is it, Sasha?" asked Kehi.

It was evident that Sasha was trying to recall this part of the forest. While Sasha scanned the area, he said, "I remember this place now. It is starting to look vaguely familiar. There is a cave... very close by, and it should be large enough for the horses too."

With the three men engaged in conversation, Shift's gaze had turned toward Salair and he kept staring at her intently. This was the first opportunity he had gotten to see her face, and he narrowed his eyes in thought. Chuck, who happened to glance in his direction, followed his gaze to the Princess. Salair saw that Shift was staring at her, so she adjusted her hood around her face and turned away from his gaze.

"Shift!" snapped Chuck and grabbed Shift by the neck, shoving him hard away from the Princess, causing him to fall. "What's your problem? Keep your eyes off my cousin?" Chuck yelled alarmingly.

"I wasn't looking at her, I... " he stammered.

"Keep your eyes to yourself, or your journey ends right here... right now!" he warned.

Chuck stared at Shift for a moment longer.

"We'll wait there for you," said Sasha, breaking the silence.

Salair hung back as the three men surrounded Shift menacingly while he remounted Shia.

"You'll be blindfolded on this leg," said Chuck. "You definitely don't need to see where this cave is."

Shift didn't utter a word.

Chuck and Kehi placed Shift behind Sasha, who was now in the lead. Chuck followed Shift and behind him was Salair, who was a little shaken up by Shift's stare. However, riding with Berra made the Princess feel a little better. Kehi brought up the rear.

Sasha came to a stop not very far from Drouck's forecastle. "This is it," called Sasha, bringing Sleet to a halt. He jumped from his saddle and rushed to push branches, brush and debris aside to reveal a rather large entrance into the cave.

Sasha lit a very small fire to lighten up the cave. "Ally, come inside. We'll get the rest. Come sit by the fire."

"Thanks," she said gratefully, as she wanted to get away from Shift. "I wonder if he recognized me?" she thought to herself.

"This is perfect, Sasha. Oshi, bring the horses," said Chuck. "You will be staying with the Princess, of course," Sir Charles said quietly to Sasha.

"She will not be out of my sight. I don't know if Shift recognized her or not, but we must assume he did."

"I agree."

"And will you watch after my horses and Berra? They are great protectors too so you can look after each other. Hopefully, we won't be gone long," Chuck said as he gazed at the Princess.

Berra was sitting on Shia, keeping a close watch on everyone. "Berra, my beautiful girl!" Chuck stroked her head and stated, "You will remain with everyone for their protection, yes?" Berra chirped a worried chirp and nuzzled his hand. "That's my girl."

Chuck went over to the fire where the Princess was. "Don't worry about Shift. He will never see you again. You have my word. You will be safe here with Sasha and the horses."

"Thank you, Chuck," whispered the Princess as she placed her hand in his. "Don't take too long, though, and be careful."

He squeezed her hand, reciprocating her gesture.

"Chuck, we must go," prodded Kehi.

They got outside, pulled the brush over the cave's entrance, and set off from where they came, grabbing the blindfolded Shift.

"The first thing we have to find out is if Drouck is in this castle."

"He won't be," said Shift. "I told you before that he uses this place for training purposes only. He is always at his main castle in The Dark Forest."

"Do you know where he is keeping your daughter?" Kehi inquired.

"He has made her one of his servants so she could be anywhere. We'll go through the servant's door around the back of the castle."

"What about the other servants?" Chuck asked, "Will they try to stop us?"

"No, they won't say anything. They are afraid of Drouck, and they absolutely hate him. They don't particularly like me either," he said wryly.

"What a shocker," said Chuck. "Let's go then. Lead on, Shift. The sooner we find this place and get rid of you, the better."

"Here we are again," said Chuck while lifting the blindfold off Shift's eyes.

"Stay low and behind me," instructed Shift. "There are lookouts everywhere."

As suggested, they crouched down and followed Shift in a single file, hiking about half a mile along a barely discernible dark trail. Chuck and Kehi exchanged concerned glances as they marched, unsure if Shift really knew where he was headed or even if he had a daughter. It was growing late in the evening before Shift halted, turned to them, and placed a finger against his lips for silence. He then pointed through the trees. The two men looked through the approaching darkness and could make out a dimly lit castle.

"It's late," whispered Shift, "there won't be as many guards on duty at night, so our timing is good right now."

Creeping across the meadow toward the castle just as the sun was setting, they reached the door without incident. As soon as Shift reached for the door handle, the door flew open. There stood a frightened girl with a knife to her throat. "Daddy!" she cried.

"Shut it," warned the guard, tightening the knife. "Come on in, Shift." He smiled wickedly.

Shift waved his hand behind his back, motioning for the others to stay back and out of sight. Rather than enter the open doorway, he took a couple of steps back and yelled angrily at the guard, "Let my daughter go, you coward. She hasn't done anything to you."

"No, but you have," snarled the guard.

Chuck snuck forward toward Shift, wondering how to take out the guard. Suddenly, a star flew past everyone, striking the guard's forehead and dropping him dead.

"Whoa!" cried an astonished Chuck. They all turned to see Kehi standing with a satisfied expression on his face.

"Nice work, Oshi!" Chuck exclaimed.

"Daddy!" shrieked Shift's daughter and started running towards him.

"Nia!" Shift crooned as he hugged her while the others looked on in astonishment.

"Well, I'll be," Chuck thought to himself. "He was telling the truth. I guess there is a first time for everything." Then his eyes became huge as he stared at the girl. She was beautiful! Tall and slender, her skin like ivory, her eyes a light sky blue, and her hair like a shiny black mane. Chuck turned to Kehi, who was likewise studying the girl, his mouth agape.

"Majikayo(seriously?)!" whispered Kehi in shock, meeting Chuck's gaze.

"What is going on here? Rather closely resembles someone we recently met," whispered Chuck.

"Majikayo!" Kehi exclaimed again. "The resemblance is uncanny. That's not possible?"

"That explains why Shift was staring at Salair," whispered Chuck.

"He was?" asked Kehi.

"Yes, just before we separated. There is something really off about this whole thing," said Chuck.

Shift's daughter was anxiously questioning Shift. "What are you doing here, Father? Drouck will have you killed if he finds you!" exclaimed Nia.

"I came to get you out of here, Nia. I don't care what he does to me. I could not leave you in this wretched, god-forsaken place. Now, let's not waste time and get out of here quickly. Where are all the servants?"

"They are all in the castle doing their chores. That guard happened to see you coming and grabbed me."

Shift turned the girl toward the two astonished bystanders. "What did I tell you, Chuck? This is my daughter, Nia. This is Chuck and Kehi."

The two men nodded politely, desperately trying to hide their disbelief. "This is your daughter, Shift? Your daughter?" asked Sir Charles, dumbly, with a strong emphasis on 'your'.

"Yes, she is," he mumbled nervously, giving him a short, sideways glance.

"Thank you for helping my father," said Nia. "However, I...I am sorry, but I cannot leave with you now."

"Oh yes, you can," Shift contradicted, determined to get her out of there.

"Well, there is a complication," she replied hesitantly.

"What do you mean, Nia?" asked Chuck suspiciously, wondering what other surprises lay in store for them.

"Well... please just follow me," stated the lovely young lady as she began leading them toward the deep recesses of the castle. "There is a person in the dungeon that needs our help. She was brought in a few days ago, and I've been taking care of her. She keeps her hood over her head and is very quiet."

"Who is she?" Chuck interrupted suspiciously.

"I don't know, I've never seen her face, but she must be someone very important because there are always rotating guards on her. That has never happened before, not that I know of."

Chuck and Kehi exchanged quick glances... could it be?

Nia continued, "Prince Drouck was actually here when she was brought in."

"Drouck? Here?" Sir Charles whirled on Shift defiantly. "You told us Drouck never comes here. You blasted liar!"

Nia jumped to her father's defense. "Please sir, the Prince hasn't been here for a long time, and he only comes rarely. However, it was not a coincidence that he was here when they brought her in the first day." She hesitated as if wanting to say more.

"And..." Chuck prodded. He was curious and wanted to learn more about the prisoner.

"And," she went on, "Well...he seemed so pleased that his guards had found her, but I got the impression he was expecting someone else too. He was really yelling at one of his men about his failure to get both of them. He was horrible to her. He kept yelling at her and hitting her. He wanted to know where King Sargon was – as if she would know."

Kehi looked at Chuck, who nodded barely to him. Now, they thought they knew for sure.

Nia kept the conversation going, "She told him that she didn't know anything, which enraged him even further. He told her he didn't believe her and kept on slapping her. It was awful. Now we must hurry. Drouck will be back soon. His guards are everywhere. We have to be very careful while getting to the dungeon."

"Wait," said Kehi. "We will need a distraction to get them away from the door."

"I know these guys," volunteered Shift. "It will be easy for me to distract them."

"No, Daddy! They will kill you. They think you betrayed them."

"Shift," said Chuck, ignoring Nia's pleading, "if you can lure the guards away from the door, we can take them out."

"Okay, I can do that. I just want to get Nia out of here...fast."

"Let's go then," urged Kehi.

Nia quickly led them down several dark, misty recesses until they reached a large torch burning above the desired door. They remained hidden in the darkness while Shift stepped out.

Observing an approaching shadow, a guard called out, "Who's there?"

Shift, assuming a casualness he did not feel, continued walking and called out, "Who is so important here that it must have you two cutthroats on guard?"

"Shift!" cried one guard.

"I thought you were dead!" gaped the other.

"You'll have to try again," he declared as he wheeled around and raced back to the awaiting trio.

"Get him!" cried the guard as they both ran after him.

Chuck and Kehi stepped quickly from the darken cove to stand in front of the rushing men. "Gentlemen," Chuck greeted the shocked guards a split second before he and his Japanese companion dropped them lifeless to the cold, hard floor.

"Nia, get the key... quickly!" panted Shift.

"Hurry!" urged Chuck, "We'll get rid of these two."

Nia unlatched the door key from the fallen guard's belt as Chuck began dragging him away. She then ran toward the door with Shift beside her. Chuck stood behind Nia as she was unlocking the door. Her hair was extraordinarily black, and then he noticed something that shook him a bit. The tips of her hair were exactly like Salair's. However, they were just the opposite; the ends of her hair were white. This was just too coincidental. And then he noticed something even more perplexing. The ends of her hair had taken on a slight glow.

“What could that mean?” he thought. “Something is terribly wrong here,” he muttered to himself.

A click disrupted his thoughts as Nia swung the door open.

CHAPTER 7

As they entered the dungeon, not only was it damp and cold, but a rancid smell wreaked throughout. Clearly this had to be the worst part of the castle. A cloaked figure huddled in the corner. The figure struggled to stand and backed even closer against the wall. Chuck approached slowly. Though he could not see her face, he simply assumed she must be Queen Victoria.

Chuck spoke very respectfully in a low, soothing voice. "Excuse us Madam, but we are here to help you." I am Sir Charles, and this is Kehi. He motioned towards his friend who was standing by the opposite wall. "Perhaps you remember us?"

Nia noticed how respectful Chuck was toward the woman. This was slightly perplexing for her. "How could they know this woman?" she thought to herself.

The woman partially unveiled her face to see everyone more clearly.

Chuck continued, "We don't have much time. We came to rescue this young woman, and she told us you had been brought here as well. We must get you out of here immediately."

"Please, Madam," chimed in Nia. "They are telling the truth. There is no time to waste."

The woman looked intently at Chuck. "Yes, of course! I remember you. I'm sorry, I'm a bit shaken up. It's nice to see a friendly face," she said with a faint smile.

"Someone is in the hall," murmured Kehi.

"Want me to bring them in here to you?" Nia whispered, remembering how easily they had disposed of the guards. "I can tell them something is wrong," added Nia.

"Good idea," agreed Chuck. "Madam, let's get you back to the corner please."

The woman obeyed. They all backed up by the door against the wall.

"Help, help! Somebody help me!" She shouted frantically from the doorway.

Two guards came running down the hall as quickly as possible. "What is it?" asked one.

"Hey," said the other guard. "How did you get in here? You don't have a key!" growled the other, glaring angrily at Nia.

Nia backed up towards the Queen and, ignoring the latter, said with urgency in her voice, "Something is wrong with this woman."

"What do you mean?" asked the guard. "You didn't answer my question!" Nia was standing inside the room just out of the guard's reach.

"Come here!" said one of the guards as he stepped into the room.

"No!" said Nia, backing up.

"I said, come here!" As the guard stepped into the room, trying to grab Nia. "Take her!" said the second guard while stepping in.

"I don't think so." Kehi and Chuck rushed toward the guards, knocking them out cold.

"Nice work, Nia," nodded Kehi.

"Tie and gag them, Shift," ordered Chuck. "Use those ropes over there."

Shift just wanted to take Nia and get out of there, but he obeyed.

"That should have bought us a bit of time," said Nia. "This is getting too dangerous for all of us."

"Let's go," said Chuck. "Nia, get us out of here. Hurry."

"Nia," barked Shift, "stay behind me."

"Kehi, you get behind Nia. Madam, follow Kehi, and I will watch out for you," ordered Chuck.

The Queen took a couple of steps behind Kehi and fell. "Oh dear," whispered Nia as she turned around.

"I've got this," said Chuck. "Keep going, Nia. I've got her."

"I am sorry. I haven't had much food or water. I am a little weak."

"Oh geez!" exclaimed Kehi. "I've got her, Chuck. Just watch our backs. Let me help you," he said and scooped the Queen up."

"Okay Kehi, let's get to the servant quarters, and then I believe I can take it from there."

"Thank you," she smiled.

"Let's go!" said Shift. "Stay behind me, Nia."

Shift led them out of the gloomy cell into an even more dreary passageway. Eerie, dark shadows danced off damp, dimly lit walls caused by the burning of infrequent torches. "Keep together," Shift whispered.

After what seemed like hours of stealth, though they were only a few anxious minutes, they reached the servant quarters with no incident.

"Are you okay? Let me set you down," said Kehi, carefully setting her on a crude wooden bench.

"I'm fine," she said wearily.

"Go guard the door Shift so this woman can rest a minute," Chuck ordered.

Shift just wanted to get out of there but didn't want to cross Chuck. "Right," Shift said and went over to guard the door without paying any attention to the woman they just rescued.

Walking over to the woman, Chuck whispered to her, "Queen Victoria, we must get you to safety. There are guards everywhere. Will you be able to go on?"

"Yes, I can, Chuck." She partially lowered her hood off, revealing her bruised face.

Nia was standing next to Chuck and was most curious about the exchange between the two. For the last couple of weeks, she had been assisting a shrouded, frail figure, totally ignorant of her identity. The guards only allowed her to place food and water inside the door where she had surreptitiously whispered positive words of kindness and encouragement to the abused and unknown person. Now, Nia stared, transfixed at the exposed face of the Queen; varied feelings and emotions flooded her mind. "I know her! But how could I? Yet I do! Something about her is familiar to me. She is beautiful and regal. But who could she be?"

Chuck's brisk voice broke the spell, "Your Highness, we must get you to safety. I am afraid we have little time. Can you stand?"

Nia looked from one to the other in confusion. He had called her "Your Highness?" Who was she?

"I'm bruised and beaten, but I will do whatever is necessary to get away from here and that awful creature that kept hitting me and asking me where my husband was."

"I'm so sorry, Madam," blurted Nia, in sincere sympathy for the brutality the Queen had suffered. "I wish I could have stopped them."

"That's quite alright, my dear. There's nothing you could have done. You saved me, though, by bringing Chuck and Kehi to me. Come here, let me see you." Nia came over to see the Queen. The hood fell back off her head, spilling her black hair down the front of her while still keeping her head down.

"Nia, could that be you?"

"I'm not sure what you mean Your Highness," whispered Nia. "I'm just a servant."

"I had a daughter named Nia. Where did you come from," said the Queen, squeezing Nia's hand and stroking her hair. "Let me see your face." They looked at each other for the first time. There was something very familiar about this woman in front of her, but Nia didn't know what it was.

The ends of Nia's hair were glowing again. "My god! This can't be possible!" said the Queen, grabbing the ends of her own hair, which were also glowing. "How did you come by this girl? She doesn't belong to you!" The Queen snapped at Shift, furious for an answer. Shift turned around and saw Nia holding the Queen's hand.

"Someone is coming! We need to get out of here... NOW! Come, Nia! Quickly!" He grabbed Nia's other hand, yanked her away from the Queen, and rushed her out into The Dark Forest. Nia glanced helplessly over her shoulder at the Queen and was struck by the anguished expression on the Queen's face.

"Stop them!" cried the Queen, struggling to go after them, taking a few steps after them and falling. "Come back! Please come back!"

Kehi ran to the servants' door and looked into the hallway. "No one is coming. Why did he say that?"

"Oshi, get Shift!" Chuck commanded.

Kehi ran out the door after Shift.

With tears welling in her eyes, Queen Victoria looked at Chuck, "Not again, not again!"

"I'm sorry Your Highness...not again?" asked Chuck. "He claims he is her father, and she refers to him as such." Then he looked questioningly at the dismayed Queen, "I am reluctant to intrude, but what is going on here? You saw her. She looks exactly like Salair, only with black hair. How is that possible?"

"That rat is not her father! She looks like Salair because Nia is her twin sister! Then, as if whispering to herself, she mumbled, "My precious Nia, I knew you were alive. Finally, I have found you."

Kehi burst into the room. "They're gone. No sign of them."

Kehi looked at Chuck's face first and then at the Queen's.

"What is it?" he asked.

"Nia is Salair's twin sister," said Chuck.

"We must find her," repeated the Queen resolutely as she wiped away the tears.

"We will find her, Your Highness," vowed Chuck. "I promise you; we WILL find her."

"Yes, we will," reiterated Kehi, "but right now, there's a bunch of commotion echoing down the hall. They have undoubtedly discovered your disappearance, my Queen. We've got to get out of here immediately. No offense, but you are of the utmost importance right now. "

They quickly weighed their options. "It sounds like they are sending more men outside, so maybe it would be wise for us to wind our way around inside. They would not be expecting that." Chuck's battle instincts kicked in.

"Wise idea, sir."

"Lead the way, Oshi. With your tracking and escaping skills, we are in good hands."

"Will you be able to walk, Your Highness? Otherwise, I can carry you until you are strong enough to run on your own."

"Thank you, Chuck. I will need some help for now."

"Of course." Chuck scooped her up in his arms and followed Kehi. They stayed in the gloomy passage and hurried along its dreary route, jumping twice into darkened alcoves to avoid being caught. The Queen, Chuck realized, was in considerable pain but bravely refrained from verbalizing it.

"How will I explain this to Salair?" murmured the Queen, her mind on what she considered way more important than the extreme discomfort of the jarring she was enduring.

"She is waiting for us in a cave up ahead," he said, growing a bit tired of the darkened hallways now.

"In a cave? How is that possible? By herself?"

Chuck was forced to smile at the Queen's persistence. "She's with Sasha, Your Highness. She is safe." Chuck whispered reassuringly.

Kehi stopped and turned around, warning them with his finger to his lips. They became silent. Their feet barely brushed the dirt floors, making the only noise. At last, they saw rays of moonlight outlining a door ahead of them. When they reached it, Sir Charles let the Queen stand, shaking his arms to revive the circulation.

"How are you feeling now, Your Highness?"

"Much better, surprisingly," adrenaline rush, she surmised.

Kehi cracked the door, careful not to allow what little light the forest had to offer to flow inside the darkened hallway. He scanned the outside area, then reported, "I don't see anything. Let's go."

As the Queen stepped forward on her own, each man grabbed an elbow to assist her. Kehi kicked the door shut behind them as they ran towards the closest trees in the forest. Just as they gained shelter behind a large spreading fir, they heard shouting from the castle.

"Spread out, search the area! They can't be far!"

They quickly plunged into the depths of the forest. Thankfully, with the help of the moonlight that night, Kehi was able to follow Shift's footprints from their journey to the forecastle.

"Nice," he thought to himself, "This way."

Queen Victoria was gallantly trying to walk as fast as she could and not detain the men. Chuck appreciated her efforts and, with a pang of guilt, thought of her torment at having found Nia after so many years only to lose her again. He regretted not having stopped Shift from grabbing Nia and disappearing in the thick dark forest, but he obviously had no way of really knowing Nia's connection to the Queen or Shift. In agitation, he looked around at the shadowy, dreary forest. No wonder Drouck had his training camp here. No one could find anything in this depressing place. It was gloomy and dark – just like Drouck. He vowed to bring Oshi back and take this place down.

Kehi tugged them to a halt and whispered, "Hear that?" Branches were swishing and cracking behind them. "Keep going, sir. Get the Queen out of here. I will take care of it." With that, he silently slipped into the darkness.

"Your Highness, if I could have your hand so we don't get separated. I think the cave we are looking for is just up there." Chuck said, encouraging her onward, knowing she was injured and fatigued. The cave should be just ahead of us."

"I hear something," Sasha called to Salair. "Stay with the horses. If anything happens and I don't return, ride out of here with them and head back to Chuck's castle."

"Sasha, look!" Salair pointed at the ends of her hair, which had started glowing.

"That's odd, it means your mother is nearby? Not possible Salair."

"It's never wrong Sasha."

"I'll be back," he said as he raced out of the cave.

He hurried from the cave, sword in hand, and soon observed two ghostly figures approaching. He crouched behind a bush, waiting to see if he could recognize them. As they drew closer, he could not believe his good fortune. "Chuck," he hissed rather loudly, "over here." As they approached, he recognized the second person. "My word, Your Highness, what in the world! Salair was right. Hurry, follow me." Chuck held onto the Queen's arm for support as they hurried behind Sasha to return to the cave. Just as they stepped into the cave's entrance, the Queen collapsed.

"I'm sorry," she groaned, "I'm just a bit weak." She was trying to put on a brave face as much as possible in front of everyone despite her extreme pain and exhaustion.

"Mother!" shouted Salair, running over to help her mother. "What in the world happened? What are you doing here?" looking questionably at Chuck. "Where is Kehi?"

Sasha and Chuck carried the Queen into the cave for safety and gently set her down.

Chuck said, "Drouck's men were getting too close. He went back to take care of them... Sasha, if you can manage here. I don't want to leave Kehi out there without any help." Just as Chuck turned around to leave...

"Not necessary, Chuck." Kehi entered the cave with a stern look on his face. We did have a couple of them coming up on us. Not anymore."

"Never doubted you for a minute, Kehi. Just thought I would watch you in action," Chuck said jokingly but gravely relieved. "Let's give it a bit to make sure there's no one else around for us to run into. Besides, the Queen needs a bit of rest." He glanced around the cavern. "Sasha, you were right; this cave is very well hidden. It took us a while to find it."

"It was a mainstay for my mother and I when we went into hiding. I'm surprised no one has found it, but relieved for us right now."

Chuck looked over at Salair. At least she was safe for now, but there were a multitude of questions bothering him. Did Salair know about Nia? He dared not say a word. Information such as this must come from her mother.

"Mother," Salair murmured as she held her hand, "what happened to you?" Then, turning towards Chuck, she asked, "Chuck, where did you find her? I thought you went with Shift to find his daughter. Instead, you return with my mother?"

"Salair, your mother was imprisoned by Drouck where Shift's uh…'daughter' was held. She helped us get your mother out." He didn't want to say too much more.

"So, Drouck did this to you mother?" the enraged Salair asked.

"Yes, Salair." The Queen didn't want to talk about it. Changing the subject, she asked, "How did you get here? Why are you with Chuck and Kehi?"

"When it was discovered you and father were missing, Sasha came to me and told me about the emergency instructions father had given him a few years ago. The directions were fairly cryptic, and it took some time to decipher, but as you see, everything worked out.

"Your father and Chuck are great friends. I have not seen you in a very long time," the Queen said, glancing at Chuck admirably.

"But where's father? How did you get separated?"

"Your father wasn't with me. He left for the Ironwood Castle the minute he received word that Christian had found a rare flower in The Black Forest."

Berra heard The Black Forest and astonished them all by flying a rapid circle around the room, whistling a very low, dark sound.

Chuck looked up in bewilderment and exclaimed, "Whoa Berra, what? Here girl!" Chuck held out his arm for Berra to land on. He tried soothing her, stroking her head to reassure her and eyeing her with a perplexed expression.

Kehi was also puzzled at Berra's behavior. "That was unusual for Berra," he said. "I've never heard that dark note."

"I am sorry I have upset Berra." The Queen hurried to apologize. "She obviously knows something about the... uh... that forest."

Salair was not interested in Berra's odd behavior; her mind was still on their earlier conversation.

"But mother," Salair continued, "if you and father weren't together, how did you end up being captured?"

"I would rather not talk about that right now," said the Queen as she looked away. It was evident to all that the Queen was in great distress, and they grew silent.

"I'm sorry, mother, it's a lot right now."

After a few moments, she composed herself and continued. "It was a closely held secret that Sargon was going to Ironwood. We wanted everyone to think we were going to the castle in the prairie lands." She glanced at the Captain of the Royal Guards.

"Sasha, I do apologize for keeping this from you, but the King believed that sharing this information would put you and Salair in grave danger. Everyone must understand the discovery of this flower is, perhaps, the most important event of our lifetime. The fewer people know about this, the better, especially if word got out, the dark creatures would waste no time hunting it down."

"Understood, Your Highness," Sasha remained silent, feeling a bit betrayed. He was, after all, the Captain of the Royal Guards and entrusted with Salair.

Chuck was focused on the Queen's revelation and asked, "How so, Your Majesty?"

"The forest I was just talking about used to be The Valley of Waterfalls and Flowers. The greatest forest of our time. That flower heralds from this forest and this forest only."

Again, Berra interrupted with a loud and happy melody. The Queen was puzzled until Chuck related that they had mentioned this valley before, and Berra sang at the mere mention of it.

"I'm quite sure that was the same tune she sang the very first time we mentioned the valley," Kehi added.

Chuck looked at his unique bird. "Berra, do you know The Valley of the Waterfalls and Flowers, girl?" Again, Berra broke into the same melody.

"It is obvious that Berra knows something about this. Finding this rare turquoise flower may be the key to reviving The Lost Forest."

"Wait a minute, you mean The Lost Forest is real?" Kehi said in disbelief.

"Why yes Kehi, and the finding of the turquoise flower proves it. This flower goes back to ancient times and possesses powers that we still are unsure about. That's why we had to be so secretive. The mere fact that the King's brother, Christian, got out alive with this flower is a miracle in itself. But I caution you, this must be kept secret. We would put the King and Christian in grave danger if this were to become known."

"That's incredulous!" exclaimed Kehi.

"I would say, judging by Berra's reaction, she seems to maybe have a distinct tie to that forest and the valley, but what is the mystery?" said Chuck.

"That forest," the Queen went on, "was taken over by the darkest factions imaginable. My husband and I thought there was no hope for recovery as far as The Black Forest was concerned. This flower could only come from the original Lost Forest, hence The Black Forest. I think they are one and the same. It is the only answer."

Again, Berra interrupted with a low, dark whistle.

"Wait mother," interjected Salair, "did you say that flower Uncle Christian found was turquoise?"

"Why yes, Salair, why?" inquired the Queen.

"Watch." Salair went to Berra and looked directly into her eyes. She seemed to lapse into a trance, and once again, the bird's feathers and Salair's eyes assumed the eerie turquoise glow.

"That's impossible. I don't understand," exclaimed the Queen. "This is an amazing revelation. Dare I say that Berra came from The Lost Forest?"

"With the information you just shared, and judging by her reactions and demeanor," interrupted Kehi, "that is highly possible."

"I would say so," said Chuck, "and who took her and either saved her, or left her to die, we are still trying to figure out."

Sasha glanced at Salair and noticed she was just staring into space. "Salair, Salair!" Waiving his hand in front of her eyes.

"Yes, Sasha?" she replied, blinking hard to snap out of her trance.

"Are you all right, daughter?"

"Yes, but I saw something, something dark with a lot of legs and bright red eyes."

"A spider, perhaps?"

"Yes, but... different... an octopus-like creature," shivered the Princess. "Not sure what that means."

"That's crazy," said Kehi as he picked up on that description, "an octospy. Perhaps you saw an octospy. They are the result of breeding a spider with an octopus. Nasty creatures. Remember, Chuck?"

At these words, Berra cocked her head and emitted several horrible cries as if she knew exactly what the conversation was and remembered a disturbing event.

Berra's cry alarmed Chuck. She was still perched next to Chuck. "Berra, what is it? I'm so sorry girl. Nothing will happen to you again, you know that," he said while stroking her beautiful, feathered back.

A now calm and contented Berra whistled a note of concurrence.

"With that reaction Oshi, I'm wondering if those creatures kidnapped Berra and somehow dropped her unknowingly."

"Maybe, Chuck. But she was stuck in that spider web. Maybe they left her there intentionally? But why would be my question."

"Chuck, looks like we are slowly finding out something of importance with Berra's past," Kehi noted. "What I find interesting is the first time Salair and Berra looked at each other, you said you saw a turquoise flower, correct, Salair?"

"Why yes, Kehi, that's true, and the second time, I also went into a trance and saw the turquoise flower again. It feels more like a vision now instead of a trance."

"So Salair, without knowing exactly what it meant, you saw the turquoise flower that Christian rescued from that forest," remarked the Queen.

"Wow. That's right, Your Highness," said Chuck. "Maybe Berra is trying to tell us something through Salair? Even more to figure out now. Visions can sometimes be helpful or harmful. But right now, we must leave and get to safety. I am sure there will be another round of soldiers coming."

"Yes, of course," agreed Queen Victoria, staring at both of them, "and I must thank you both, but we have work to do."

"Indeed, there is, Your Majesty." Sir Charles nodded as he and Kehi exchanged understanding glances.

"Where is Shift anyway?" Sasha asked, having completely forgotten about their former prisoner. "Did he really have a daughter?"

"Well… uh…," Sir Charles was evasive. "He grabbed the girl and lit out for the forest. We lost track of him. He undoubtedly wanted to get her as far from Drouck as possible while he had the chance." Then he added quietly, "And us."

Kehi observed Chuck struggling to avoid the conversation and tried to steer it in a different direction. "The best thing that came out of this was finding you, Your Highness," Kehi asserted sincerely, nodding to the Queen.

Salair was not to be deterred, "I can't even guess what state of mind that poor girl was in. She must be so relieved to be with her father once again."

"I can assure you; Nia is not Shift's daughter," snapped the Queen.

"Who's Nia, mother?" asked Salair. "The girl? How would you know she is not Shift's daughter?"

"I would know because Nia is my daughter and your twin sister," she said bluntly.

Salair's mouth dropped in shock. There was silence. Chuck and Kehi stood by quietly and sympathetically. Sasha was also mute, thinking.

Then finally, Salair managed, "What do you mean, Mother? My... twin... sister? I'm not sure what to say. Shift took her?"

"Shift grabbed her and disappeared back into the forest before Kehi could stop him," explained Chuck.

"I have lost her again," the Queen choked up and could say no more.

"We'll do everything in our power to get her back, Your Highness. Mark my words," assured Chuck.

"I'm sorry everyone, but we must get moving immediately," interrupted Kehi.

Salair gave Chuck a confused smile, fought back a rising anger, and approached her mother with tears in her eyes.

"Mother, I am sure this is very painful for you, but you must tell me everything when we get to safety. I need to know. How could you have kept it from me all these years? A twin sister?"

"My dear, you cannot imagine how this has haunted me. When you were a child, you were too young to understand. As you grew older, it became more complicated, especially since I thought Nia was dead. I didn't want to hurt you. Please forgive me." She got very quiet.

"I'm sorry, Mother. You are right. There's no way I could imagine what a nightmare this has been for you and father. I'm just flabbergasted, I guess."

The three men stood awkwardly by, eager to be moving. Even Berra remained quiet throughout the drama.

"Believe me, Salair, when Kehi and I first saw Nia, there was no mistaking that you two are related. I know this is a lot for everyone right now," said Chuck, "but we really must get out of here. The longer we wait, the better chances of us being caught." Chuck looked over at Salair. She looked back at him with a thankful but painful smile.

"Well, at least we know where Drouck's training camp is," said Kehi uncomfortably.

Sir Charles grabbed the opening, "Yes, indeed, and Sasha, when we're able, we need to get word to the King about its location."

"Absolutely, we do," replied Sasha.

"Also," continued Chuck, "we need to capture that castle and start reclaiming some land. If we don't, Drouck will keep doing what he's obviously been doing for a while now – quietly taking over land bit by bit. He aims to have the entire forest – and ruin it, just like what he and the others did to The Valley of the Flowers and Waterfalls." Again, Berra sang her song.

"There she goes again." Kehi shook his head in bewilderment.

"I know, Berra. We'll figure it out girl, I promise," said Chuck as he glanced toward the very unique bird. Berra flew over and landed on Chuck's shoulder, nudging the side of his face with her beak.

"Oshi, check the perimeter and see if it's safe to leave."

"Absolutely." Kehi stepped out of the cavern. After several minutes, he returned, "Looks pretty quiet. We should go now."

Chuck and Sasha readied the horses for another leg of the trip, giving Salair and her mother time to absorb the shock of the unexpected events and regain their composure.

"I'm sorry, my darling," the Queen whispered to Salair. "I know this is a lot for you with everything else right now, but when we get to safety, you can ask me whatever you want. The whole thing is just so shocking. I never expected to see my precious Nia again."

"I'm sorry too, mother. I can't imagine what it has been like for you and father. But I would love to know anything you can tell me. We will find my sister. I believe in my heart; she will be with us again one day and our family will be whole again."

The Queen looked at Salair with tears welling up in her eyes. "Oh Salair, thank you for your heartfelt words," she said as she hugged her daughter. "We will stop at nothing and find her."

"All right," said Chuck, "Kehi will lead out and keep a watchful eye on our surroundings. Your Highness, you and Salair will ride Shia. Sasha, you follow them, and I will bring up the rear."

"Let's do it," said Sasha. "Once we are clear of this dark place, I will go in front and lead us to my friend, the fuzzar." They helped the Queen onto Shia, and Salair rode with her. Everybody else walked back in silence along the path they had come from. There was an eerie silence in the forest, which gave Salair the creeps. She swore she saw red eyes peering at them. After about an hour of creeping along, they finally saw some sunlight ahead of them. "Thank god Shia," whispered Salair.

Knowing exactly what she meant, her mother agreed, "It is indeed a welcome sight, dear."

Chuck pulled Sleet to an abrupt halt. "What is it?" Sasha asked.

"I'm not sure. I thought I heard something." Chuck held his horse very still, as did Sasha. Once more, they heard a rustling sound behind them. "There it is again. Hear it?" Berra let out a very low warning chirp. "I know, girl. This forest is hard to get through, but we need to hurry now."

"I have a very bad feeling," said Kehi.

"I swear, I saw red eyes staring at us," said the Princess.

"Like your vision, Princess."

"Yes, Kehi."

Suddenly, Chuck shouted, "Oshi, lead us out, and fast! We've got to get out of here now!"

"Let's go!" Kehi spurred Tarr into a fast gallop. Their powerful horses bore the heavy burden of plowing rapidly through thick underbrush and pushing aside sharp branches while their razor-sharp hooves easily slashed through the forest. They had only fifty yards left to sunlight when Salair anxiously glanced behind her, "Chuck, what is that?"

"If that's what I think it is, we've got to keep moving!" Chuck grimly shouted. There were pairs and pairs of red eyes closing in on Chuck and company. "Hurry, Kehi!" cried Chuck.

"Push the horses faster! Everyone, follow me!"

The gallant steeds raced wildly toward the sunlight – all except for Sleet, who wheeled around to face a giant red spider. "Easy boy." Sir Charles was muttering as Sleet had his own ideas about how to treat this menace. He reared high in the air, surprising Chuck, who grabbed for the saddle horn; then his sharp hooves landed like granite, slashing the spider in half. Out of nowhere, another spider darted toward Sleet, who whirled and sent that one sailing with his back hooves. More were coming now. Berra was soaring above Chuck, crying out for Sleet to retreat. Chuck jabbed his heels into the white steed, urging him into the sunlight. "Let's go, you two. There's too many of them now." Several of the deadly spiders chased after the group, only to meet the same brutal death under the merciless rays of the brilliant sun, while others could only watch them get away.

CHAPTER 8

Octimus, the leader of the Octospy Nation, created a family of like species. Each spider-like species had its own unique lethal characteristics designed to torture and destroy its enemy. One of those creations is his red spider. One scratch or bite from them injects a deadly poison into its victim. This poison makes its way to the heart, resulting in a painfully tortuous death.

The red spiders watched the golden bird fly off into the sunlight with the others. "Did you see that? That was the golden bird!" whispered Fang to the others.

"It can't be!" snapped Cecil. "We have always been told that one of Octimus' octospies snatched the bird from its nest, carried it off, and then killed it."

"Well, obviously that didn't happen. I am sure that was THE bird."

"If that bird still exists, then why are our forests still thriving?"

"I can't answer that, but we need to get word to Octimus. We must find that bird and kill it; otherwise, our very existence is at stake."

"How are we going to find that bird? We don't even know who the bird was with and where they were going," Cecil responded.

"If I didn't know better, Cecil, the two women with them were the Queen and her daughter. I am pretty certain about it."

"What would they be doing in our forest? The whole thing doesn't make any sense."

"From what I've heard, the Queen was imprisoned by Drouck. How they knew she was there or found Drouck's camp is inexplicable."

"And why would the Queen's daughter be with them?"

"Right? Something very suspicious is going on Cecil. We better get word to Octimus. Once it gets dark, let's see if we can find where their tracks lead."

CHAPTER 9

Salair, who was anxiously observing the actions of Sir Charles and Sleet, heard her mother's low groan and pleaded, "Please, Mother, hang on." The sunlight was within arm's reach when she said, "I'm so sorry."

"Hurry, Salair, we must keep going," she said as she took a few deep breaths.

Kehi noted the Queen enduring the pain and shouted to Sasha, "Are we close to your friend's house?"

"Yes, it's just ahead of us," he responded. Are you alright, Your Highness? It's just up here."

The Queen gathered her strength and placed her hand on Salair's shoulder. Salair knew her mother was ready to move forward.

"Hurry, Sasha. She's fine. Let's get out of here. We're all in danger out in the open like this."

Kehi and Sasha started to take off with Salair and the Queen when they noticed something was going on with Chuck and Sleet.

"Sasha, go ahead. I'll go see what is happening. We'll catch up."

"Okay, but hurry, the manras will be after us now."

"Come on, boy," said Chuck, and as he looked down, he noticed that Sleet's hoof and leg veins were starting to turn black. He had started limping. "Dear god," he mumbled under his breath.

"Chuck, hurry! What's going on?" cried Kehi as he galloped up.

"Hang in there, Sleet. Oshi, Sleet's hurt! He got slashed by one of those red spiders."

"Oh no! Sleet!" exclaimed Salair as she glanced back at Sleet, who was limping badly now.

"Up ahead, Chuck. It's right here," prodded Sasha as they made their way to the fuzzar's house.

But Chuck was more concerned with his priceless horse than safety for himself. He dismounted and allowed Sleet to pick its own pace as he walked beside him, sword drawn.

Kehi dismounted and walked with Chuck and Sleet for protection. Sleet's leg looked bad, but Kehi didn't want to say anything because Chuck was already alarmed.

"Mother, I am sorry, but we must keep moving for a few more minutes," Salair pleaded with her injured mother.

"Sasha, we must wait for them," said the Queen. Salair came to a stop and dismounted her horse, with Sasha following suit.

"Over here," Sasha called out to them while entering another forest. Thankfully, they were now wading through tall grass, allowing some cover from the oncoming danger. "Stay down and keep a look out for the manras. I bet they must have heard the spiders scream. Between that and the Queen's disappearance, they'll be swarming the forest for us."

"Quickly everyone, it's just up here!" shouted Sasha.

"Sleet can't run. His leg is bad. You shouldn't have waited for us," stated Chuck.

"It wasn't an option," said Sasha as he glanced at the Queen. Follow me as fast as you can. I know this part of the forest well. We're near the fuzzar now. He'll know what to do to help Sleet."

Chuck was not only worried for the Queen and Salair but also for his priceless Arabian.

"Hurry, Sasha. Kehi, guard the ladies with your life. I'll catch up. We can't risk the Queen and Salair being caught. I'll ride Willow. Go now!"

"Right! But Chuck, hurry. I can see something in the distance. They don't act like they've spotted us yet. Hurry, my friend, we don't have much time."

"Let's go!" cried Sasha as they all took off except for Chuck.

Holding Willow to a slower pace, Chuck tried to accommodate the injured Sleet, who was doing his best to make it. Willow was nodding his head up and down to encourage his friend. To avoid being seen by the approaching manras he stayed in as much cover as possible while keeping his party in sight. He was extremely worried about his precious Sleet. He was a tough, resilient animal, but he had never been bitten by such a strange creature. The amount and type of poison he had absorbed was unknown, as was the effect it would have on the stallion. He was slowing down a great deal. "Come on, my boy, I know you are hurt, but you can make it." Berra was sitting on his saddle, singing an odd melody. Strangely enough, it seemed to soothe him a bit. Sleet looked at Chuck with gloomy eyes. The poison was making its way up his veins. His leg was turning blacker and more swollen by the minute; it scared Chuck. He had never seen that look in his eye.

Chuck felt sure that he could use his own wits to get himself and his two priceless Arabians to safety. As a last resort, he knew his friend, the Samurai, would return for them. He again studied Sleet's injured leg and stared into the animal's weary eyes – it further alarmed him. It would be unthinkable to lose Sleet. He was further dismayed to find that, a short distance ahead, Kehi and the others were waiting for him.

"Chuck, are you guys okay?" the Princess asked, concern written all over her face. Her mother looked worriedly, not at Chuck, but at Sleet.

"You should have gone on!" Chuck admonished. "Oshi, Sasha, why didn't you keep them moving?"

"We are not leaving anyone behind," stated the Queen.

"They refused to go," stated Kehi.

"It's just up here now," said Sasha.

With visible relief, Sir Charles patted Sleet's neck. "Hear that boy, we made it. Stay with me, my beauty. We'll get you some help soon."

"Chuck, go ahead with the others," Kehi urged. "I'll stay back a bit, just in case."

"Thank you, Oshi. I'll come back for you. Be careful, my friend. Take Berra with you." Chuck rested a hand on Kehi's shoulder for a moment, aware of the monumental risk his long-time friend was willing to take.

"Get out of here, Chuck," Patting his grandfather's sword. The Japanese warrior watched them depart. With Berra perched on his shoulder, he turned back to thwart their deadly pursuers. Chuck glanced back just in time to see Berra's feathers turning dark red.

CHAPTER 10

Sasha was trying to hurry but moved the horses slowly, being considerate of the suffering Queen and the maimed stallion.

At last, they all heard an excited Sasha proclaiming, "Here! This is the edge of The Magic Forest – a place where things happen that you won't believe or trust your eyes. This is the spot. Come this way. Trust me, this will not seem possible. See that wall of leaves right there? Quickly, form a line." They all followed Sasha's instructions, looking perplexed. "Now, have your horses take fifteen steps forward."

Salair didn't dare look at her mother, knowing she would only see disbelief mingled with impatience. She simply said, "Whatever you say, Sasha." She nudged Shia forward and began counting steps, thinking it rather silly herself. However, she was desperate to get over whatever this was as quickly as possible. Her only aim at that moment was to bring relief to her mother and Sleet. Sir Charles, displaying just a tad bit of irritation, brought his mounts into line, following the count.

"That's right, keep coming," coaxed Sasha, guiding Mirka toward the leafy obstruction. They rode straight ahead, directly at what appeared to be a rigid, solid wall of leaves. A giant breeze unexpectedly arose, violently swirling leaves around them as if they were in the midst of a tornado. Startled, the horses reared up as the wind replaced the leaves precisely into a solid wall behind them.

"Whoa, Sasha!" cried Salair, staring back at the leaf wall. "You were right, that was bizarre. So, no one can see us right now?"

"No, but let's hurry. Everyone is safe. We can go and find my friend, the fuzzar. They dismounted, except for Salair and her mother, and walked slower now as they were now safe from the deadly manras, hoping Kehi would also be. They walked their mounts at a slow, quiet pace, hoping to ease the pain the Queen and Sleet were enduring. It took a little longer than Sasha wanted, but finally, he said, "Wait, I think this is it. You would not even know it was a house unless you knew Keewae."

"I don't see anything," whispered Chuck.

"Exactly, but trust me, it is here. Keewae's house is constructed from chameleon leaves. They constantly change colors depending on the varying amount of sunlight in the forest, making it an excellent camouflage."

"So, that is what we just rode through?" asked Salair, beginning to appreciate her leafy surroundings. The Queen remained quietly appreciative as she glanced around.

"Exactly, my dear," Sasha said and pulled on one particular leaf, which was slightly different than the others (but then again, Salair couldn't tell the difference). After some rustling, the leaves started swirling again, this time tossing and pinning Sasha and Chuck to the ground.

"Who are you, and how did you get in here?" bellowed a rough, raspy voice. Salair and her mother froze. There was now a furry creature, appearing out of nowhere, with an unusually long claw standing over her friends.

"Why are you snooping around my house?" the voice roared again, this time in an even more menacing tone.

Sasha could feel the sharp claw up against the back of his neck and hoped the fuzzar remembered him. "Keewae, it's Sasha, your old friend," he mumbled as loudly as possible through the pile of leaves covering his body. Keewae slashed the leaves away from Sasha's face with surprising skill.

"My word!" exclaimed Keewae. "What in the name of the King are you doing here?" He finished cutting through the thick leaves that had engulfed Sasha and Chuck.

Breathing a sigh of relief, Sasha and Keewae briefly placed a hand and a paw on each other's shoulders. "Keewae, not to be rude, but this is the Queen and Princess of the Kingdom of The Meadow, and this here is my friend, Sir Charles. As you can see, the Queen is in bad shape, my friend's horse was bitten by some nasty spider creature, and we are being chased by Drouck's manras. We left one of our own behind so we could escape. Needless to say, we have several extreme emergencies to attend to. That's how we ended up here."

Keewae looked curiously at them while continuing his conversation with Sasha. "Let's get everyone taken care of. There is no time to waste. The spider creatures you referred to are known as octospy. Their bite or scratch can be lethal."

"Excuse me, Keewae, but those aren't the octospy I am familiar with," Chuck stated.

"There are several species of them that have morphed from the original octospy. The Black Forest probably had something to do with it, I surmise."

"Great. Just what we need."

"Sasha, take your friends that way, please," Keewae pointed toward another leafy gate. "I'll bring up the rear."

Sasha led the others through the entrance in the direction Keewae had pointed. The instant the last person, horse, and fuzzar were through, the huge bear-like character waved his paw across the entrance and another wave of swirling leaves resealed the opening they had just come through, securing them inside. He strode to the front of the group. Everyone walked behind Keewae through a hallway entirely made up of leaves. At the end of the hallway, a new leaf room appeared with a mud door on the far wall. Everyone halted in surprise when Keewae emitted two high-pitched sounds. They stood there for a few seconds before the mud door opened. There stood three smaller, younger versions of Keewae.

"Yes, Uncle?" one spoke. The intruders stared at them in amazement.

"Misa, please escort the Princess and her mother down to the house. She is in immediate need of medical help. Sasha, you will stay with the Queen and Princess. Now listen everyone, you may only enter this mud entry if you are accompanied by one of us. It would be a fatal mistake otherwise, and I do mean *fatal*. Understood?" They all nodded. "Yes, of course," said the Princess.

"If I may, my Queen? I apologize," Sasha said as he gently picked her up.

"Yes, thank you, Sasha," murmured the Queen as they followed Salair and Misa to the mud elevator. "Let's hurry," said the Princess and they disappeared down the elevator.

Keewae and his nephews hurried over to Sleet, who had collapsed. "Corga and Sin Sin, this horse has been bitten by one of those nasty red octospies. You know the salve we need. Sleet doesn't have a lot of time."

"Yes, Uncle," they chimed in unison.

"We will be right back." They raced down the elevator.

"Sir," Keewae addressed Sir Charles, "with your permission, we will tend to Sleet and the other horses. They will be fed and watered. They are in good hands with my nephews."

Chuck was standing by Sleet, his breathing labored now. He could hear a slight cry coming from him. Sleet was the toughest of the bunch, and to see him in this much pain frightened Chuck. "Sleet," Chuck stroked his face. "You're the tough one, remember?" Sleet raised his head and stared right through Chuck. "Whatever you can do to help him, I am eternally grateful," said Chuck.

"Of course," replied Keewae.

"Sasha obviously trusts you, and so shall I."

"Don't worry about the horses; they are in good hands. My nephews will be right back up."

"Ah yes, here they are." Corga and Sin Sin returned.

"Sleet is in good hands. My nephews will take care of everything. We better go and get your friend away from the manras. Follow me."

"Yes. Let's go," stated Chuck.

"Sorry for the abrupt introduction to my security system, as I call it," Keewae said with a light chuckle.

"It is quite extraordinary, to say the least. No apologies necessary."

"Just stay behind me while we get past my leaves."

Chuck followed directly behind Keewae while they walked through the foliage with the swirling leaves miraculously forming a doorway through which they both stepped.

A shrill scream rent the air.

“Hear that?” asked Keewae.

“It’s coming from over there. Let’s go!” Sir Charles ran in the direction of the scream with Keewae on his heels. They caught up to Kehi and Berra, who were spectacularly fending off five manras. Berra’s strong claws and beak made short work of one of them as she dove right at one, claws first to the face and eyes. One manra tackled the Samurai from behind, only to be grabbed by Keewae’s razor-sharp claws and flung thirty feet away, smashing him into a solid tree trunk, blood and bones flying everywhere. The warfare expert used his matchless skill with his sword to make short work of the other manras.

“Great timing guys,” grinned Kehi, brushing himself off.

“From the looks of it, I am not sure you really needed our help. Way to go, Berra,” Chuck cheered. Berra then landed on Chuck’s shoulder, let out a satisfied note, and changed back to her golden-feathered self.

“Well, that was round two, and I was getting pretty tired. Thank god Berra was with me. I have never seen her fight before. She’s frighteningly fierce.”

“I would imagine with those claws and sharp beak. That’s my girl,” Chuck admired Berra. Oshi, let me introduce you to our new friend. This is Keewae, whom Sasha spoke so glowingly about.” Bowing slightly, as composed as if he met a weird-looking beast every day, Oshi greeted, “Pleasure Keewae. Thanks for the assistance.”

"Pleasure's all mine. Now, we'd better get out of here. Let's go see how Sleet is coming, Sir Charles."

"Yes indeed," agreed Chuck in a low voice, "and if I am not mistaken, I think I hear more manras."

"They have been crawling all over the place," Kehi added.

"Let's hurry then," urged Keewae. "I don't want them near my house and must deal with that.

"Of course not." They rushed off with the fuzzar toward his leafy fortress.

Chuck found Corga kneeling beside Sleet with what looked like a doctor's medicine bag. Corga stroked his jaw. "It's okay, boy." Corga dug through his bag and pulled out a syringe, bandages, and a small jar with some stuff that resembled tar. "Sir Charles, this isn't going to feel good, so you, Sin Sin, and probably another person will need to hold Sleet down while I extract the poison. I did give him a bit of a pain killer, so that should help put him more at ease. This will still be painful."

"I'll help," Kehi agreed.

"I'll go and see how the Queen is doing," Keewae called as he slipped down the mud wall.

"Ready, gentlemen?"

"Sleet, stay put buddy." Chuck stroked his neck.

Corga bent over Sleet's hoof to get a closer look at where the bite mark was. He took out the syringe as he noticed the black poison was starting to pool around the top of his hoof. "Oh no you don't," he mumbled.

"Here we go. Keep steady, Sleet." It took everything Chuck, Kehi, and Sin Sin had to keep Sleet pinned down while Corga inserted the syringe just above the hoof. They all stared at the syringe, hoping this would work. Soon, the poison was flowing through the syringe into a pail. "Almost done, boy," he said and continued to extract the poison liquid from Sleet's hoof. Sleet was whimpering now. "Hang on, boy. Almost there." He stroked his face and neck.

"There!" Corga withdrew the needle. "Now let's get this salve on and bandage this up. This salve is a combination of a painkiller and a sedative. It's amazing stuff. The swelling in his leg should subside once that salve gets absorbed into his bloodstream. It shouldn't take too long to work all its magic."

"Will he be okay, Corga?" asked Chuck, looking for some reassurance.

"I think we got the poison out just in time. It was starting to pool around his hoof, which meant it was getting ready to spread to his heart, and that would have been it. This poison is nasty stuff, Sir Charles. You know Sleet is strong; he'll fight through it." Chuck worried, but he knew he had to have faith.

Kehi stared at the small fuzzar, then looked at Chuck. "Sleet's very tough, Chuck. He'll make it."

Then they looked over at Sleet. He looked relaxed and at peace.

"I think we can let him rest now, Sir. We'll take you down to the house. Sin Sin and I will come back up and look after your horses.

"Thank you, Corga," Chuck said while stroking Sleet's face. This was the first time they had ever encountered creatures of this kind. Sleet was not one to back down. Protecting Chuck was just in his blood. Losing Sleet was never in his plan. He hated putting one of his Arabians in this situation. They were warriors, but encountering these creatures was a new one. He couldn't bear losing any of his horses and this was the first time he came close. He went over to Tarr, Mirka, Willow and Shia. "He'll be alright boys. He is strong." They nodded in agreement. Berra, who was perched on Chuck's shoulder, flew over to Sleet and landed next to him. She gazed at Sleet and began singing a beautiful, soothing song. Everyone was shocked at what they were witnessing. Sleet's eyes got heavier and heavier until he fell asleep.

"Wow, Sir Charles, are you kidding me? I have never heard any bird sing like that!" exclaimed Corga.

"Her gift of song singing is truly remarkable and perplexing. She keeps surprising all of us!" Chuck again looked over at Kehi, who just shrugged his shoulders.

Chuck and Kehi followed Corga and Sin Sin to the mud elevator. "What is this?" asked Kehi.

"It's a mud elevator," Chuck responded. "Just make sure that you are accompanied by one of the fuzzars if you go up or down, or it will end badly for you, if you know what I mean."

"Got it."

"First time in a mud elevator, Kehi?" Corga asked as they stepped into Keewae's house. "Who hasn't ridden in a mud elevator?" joked Kehi.

The Princess, thankful for their escape from the manras, rose and rushed to greet the Samurai. "Kehi, thank you for your bravery in staying behind so we could get help for my mother. I'm indebted to you."

"It's my honor, Princess, but nothing brave about it. How is her Highness?"

"Somewhat better. She's thankful to have been rescued. She's in pretty bad shape, but she refuses to be a victim. She is a woman of character and strength, and I have always admired her for that. Misa boiled some interesting plants and made tea for her. After she drank it, her bruising disappeared, and her cuts are rapidly healing. Now, she is sleeping peacefully. That tea is nothing short of a miracle. Misa is amazing."

Bursting with pride at the nice compliments, Keewae included himself into their conversation. "Thank you, Princess. Misa is a skilled herbalist. From her studies and experiments with the unique and diverse flora varieties in our forest, she has developed a litany of antidotes to counteract the dangerous poisons that exist here – in various shapes and forms. The salve that was administered to Sleet, is a perfect example."

"That's impressive," Chuck added, "Sleet would probably be dead right now if it weren't for her."

"Well," Kehi concluded, "that is two lives you saved today, Miss Misa."

"I am only happy that my remedies were able to save the Queen and that beautiful horse. They are both very precious," Misa avowed. "But she shouldn't travel for a while. The tea needs time to work its magic."

"I don't want to impose," said Salair.

"Nonsense, I will hear none of it. She will stay." Keewae announced. "No disrespect, Your Highness."

"Thank you, Keewae, and please call me Salair."

"After what I saw Keewae, with those manras attacking me, I would very much like to remain right here," said Kehi half in jest, referring to the manras Keewae had brutally flung against a tree.

Kehi's statement drew an appreciative chuckle from the others. Salair graciously excused herself to check on her mother and then returned.

Seated comfortably in the main cave, Keewae confessed, "Actually, I was not surprised to see you all. I, along with my niece and nephews, run an underground forest information network. Our sources share information about all the happenings, if you will, in the various forests. We were informed by sources that 'people of importance' were in the forest. We had no idea they meant the Queen and Princess of The Kingdom of the Meadow. We were also told that there has been a discovery of some kind, something favorable to our forest, but that is all we know." Chuck, Salair, and Kehi all exchanged glances.

"You and your family are full of surprises, Keewae," Chuck remarked and recounted certain events. "Unseen leaf hallways, deadly mud walls, a most unusual elevator, a niece with potion powers, and now an underground information network. Very impressive, indeed!"

"Perhaps I can shed some light on that subject," said the Queen as she entered the room.

The men jumped to their feet as the Queen unexpectedly entered the room. "Mother, I thought you were sleeping. What are you doing up?"

"I am feeling much better, thanks to little Misa."

"Please sit, my Queen." Sasha got her a chair.

"I trust this to go nowhere Keewae, and thank you for keeping your word Sir Charles and Kehi. This is highly, highly secretive as I told these two. The discovery your underground network mentions is a turquoise flower. It was discovered by King Sargon's brother, Christian, in The Black Forest." Berra let out a low whistle.

"No, that can't be – a turquoise flower?" Keewae exclaimed. "That's not possible. That flower was extinguished a long time ago, on purpose, as you know."

"Well, somehow that little flower survived, and Christian has gotten it to safety," replied the Queen. "This must not get out Keewae," warned the Queen.

"Nothing leaves here without approval. We all understand this is highly secretive. I am flabbergasted by this news, my Queen. This means a revival of the most precious forest in the land."

Keewae got very quiet, soaking in this new information. My Queen, we will do whatever it takes to help you." Then he gave them further information. "The underground has word that Prince Drouck and his buddy, Octimus, are stepping up attacks around the various forests."

"The kidnapping of the Queen, the strength in numbers of the manras and spiders attacking, that explains a lot," said Kehi.

"We believe he has been in the process of rebuilding his army."

"That would make sense now, right Kehi?" inquired Chuck.

"Why yes, it would."

"What do you mean, make sense?" asked Keewae.

"Well, before you rescued us, we were led to a 'so-called training camp' by a former soldier of Drouck's."

"How did that happen?" Keewae interrupted.

"Long story short, this soldier, Shift, stumbled upon my property and was caught by my men. He proceeded to tell us that his daughter was being held captive by Drouck at this so-called 'training camp'. We didn't believe him, of course, but decided to take a chance in hopes of finding Salair's parents. So, Shift led us there to get his daughter, who turned out to be Her Majesty's daughter, Nia, and Salair's twin sister. He's the one who kidnapped her. She was trying to help the Queen without realizing she was helping her own mother. Shift tricked us while we were waiting for our opportunity to escape the camp and ran off with Nia. At that point, being surrounded by danger, we had to get the Queen to safety and, unfortunately, could not run after Nia. "And now," Chuck said with a sympathetic glance at Queen Victoria, "we vow to find Nia – again."

"Sargon won't believe it. I can't wait to tell him his daughter is alive."

"Did the Dark Prince know who she was?" asked Keewae.

"No, thank god," said the Queen. "Not the way he was treating her. He was very fond of her, but she was just a servant to him."

"Your Majesty, do you think Drouck has any knowledge about the discovery of the flower?" Sasha wondered.

"I don't think so. I think he would have let on if he knew anything. He was more angered by the fact that Sargon was not with me." She went on, "I am thinking that your underground network may come in handy."

"Anything we can do to help, Your Highness," offered Keewae. "What are your thoughts?"

"We need to get word to the King about the latest developments. I was supposed to meet him at our Forest Castle. We were to go together to get the flower to a secure location. I do not know if he is still waiting for me; obviously, I got delayed."

"Mother, I am sure he would wait, even if you did get delayed."

"Well, we had a spirited discussion on that subject. I would hope he would have gone ahead. The discovery of the flower is bigger than all of us, and we must all do our part to make sure it gets to safety."

"Well, if we are to get word to the King, the whereabouts of your castle will have to be disclosed," said Keewae.

"I am aware of that," replied the Queen, "Sargon needs to know about Nia, and if we are to ensure the safety of the flower, my precious husband, and his brother, this must be done."

"Yes, Your Highness," replied Keewae, "we will do whatever is necessary. I know everyone is tired and hungry. Misa is preparing a delicious meal for us. Let us eat and rest and make a plan in the morning. This has been quite the day of surprises, if I might say so."

"Right," agreed Kehi, intently studying the walls, "but to change the subject, I'm still trying to figure out your mud walls. Truly remarkable! How is it no one else can get through them?"

Keewae smiled and tried dodging the question. "That, my friend, is a story for later. What I will tell you is that my ancestors developed a symbiotic relationship with this mud a very, very long time ago. The mud and leaves sense any danger that might happen to me or my family. The mud will suffocate you or the leaves will strangle you, take your pick."

"I think I'll pass," grinned Sir Charles.

The Queen was studying her mud surroundings as well.

"Questions, your Majesty?" Keewae asked after noticing the Queen studying her mud surroundings.

"Oh no, Keewae. My father studied different types of plants and mud. Just brought back some memories, that's all."

Keewae got a weird feeling that there was more to that comment, but chose not to further discuss his family's protected secrets. "Interesting, your Majesty. Please excuse me while I check on Misa and our dinner," he said abruptly while getting up.

Chuck and Kehi just exchanged quizzical looks at the awkward exchange.

CHAPTER 11

Snag was a little shaken upon receiving Fang's message. Noticing his anxiousness, Octimus asked, "What's bothering you?"

"Octimus, we just received a message from Fang," Snag responded.

"Fang? Most unusual. What is it?"

"Not good, my King, it's not good. I don't know how to say this, but it seems that the golden bird is alive."

"What?!" Octimus yelled. "That's impossible. That bird was disposed of years ago. My cluster stole it from its nest and killed it. But... How does Fang know this? Is this some kind of joke?"

"He saw the bird himself. One of Fang's clusters discovered three men and two women on horseback in our forest. It appears they were in the same area as Drouck's camp. They chased after the humans, but unfortunately, they got to the sunlight before we could take them down."

"And the bird? What about the bird?" he hissed impatiently.

"While the rest of the humans ran off to the sunlight, one of the horses wheeled around to confront us. Soaring above this man and his horse was the golden bird. Fang said there was no mistaking it—golden feathers with the signature turquoise ring around her neck. One of our spiders managed to bite the horse, but to no avail. They still got away."

Octimus was silent for several minutes.

"And one more thing, my King," Snag hesitated.

"There's more?!" he boomed.

"Fang also said that one of the women riding away with the others was the Queen. He recognized her himself."

"What? Drouck was responsible for keeping the Queen's kidnapping quiet. How was she discovered? Who is she with? This is outrageous. Get word to Drouck to meet me at his camp immediately. This is such a disaster!"

"Right away, my King. But what are we going to do about the golden bird?"

"I don't know yet, but spread the word throughout our forests. That bird must be found and killed at any cost. Speaking of that, get me Tarsus. He lied to me. All those years ago, he told me he killed that bird. That liar!" he screamed. "Find him and send him to me. Get Fang to help you."

"At once, my King, at once." Snag scurried out.

CHAPTER 12

The dinner table looked magical and delightful as it was set with beautiful pottery that had an unusually odd sheen to it. Sin Sin and Misa were busily working in the kitchen while Corga tended to Chuck's horses. "Those kids are truly amazing," Salair said.

"Yes, they are," said Keewae. "Thanks to my sister. She was tragically bitten by one of those nasty spiders a few years ago and by the time we found her, the poison had spread too far. Sadly, we couldn't save her. It took a long time for us to come to grips without her."

"I can't even imagine," said Salair. "You have done a great job with them. They are wonderful."

"Too kind of you," said Keewae, "They are my pride and joy. They too, have the specialized skills that their mother was blessed with."

"What kind of skills?" asked Salair.

"Excuse me, everyone," said Misa, "dinner is ready." The aroma of the delectable food made everyone's mouth water.

"Excellent," said Keewae. "Please, after you."

Misa, an exceptional chef, prepared a caterpillar pie and beetle muffins for the fuzzars for dinner, which for them, was a huge treat. For the rest of the gang, there was a delicious spinach soup for starters, followed by a hearty stew. A large bowlful of various types of seeds and raw meat was placed in front of Berra, who happily pecked away. The most unusual aspect of the dinner was the pottery dinnerware. Just as Sasha went to say something about pouring soup on a plate, the plate transformed into a bowl. Noticing his reaction, Keewae explained that that was the uniqueness of this pottery. It contains particles from the same mud as our house. Turning it into pottery is just the beginning." Looking at Kehi, he made a throwing motion and grinned.

"No way?" said the Samurai, catching on quickly. "You mean the spiked ball you threw at the manras was made from this?" Kehi waved his plate in question.

"You got that right," smirked Keewae.

"Incredible!" Nodded Sir Charles. "The same mud as your house, you said?"

"The mud had a little developmental change, turning it into a microorganism, a highly-intelligent one. It senses its purpose at the time of use." Another scientific feat by our little Misa," Keewae boasted.

"I bet that is not the end of her scientific achievements," surmised Kehi. "Quite right," agreed the big fuzzar with a sly smile.

Everyone thoroughly enjoyed the dinner. Afterwards, the little fuzzars began cleaning the table while Keewae escorted his visitors into the den.

CHAPTER 13

As the Queen revealed, the turquoise flower was discovered and rescued by King Sargon's brother, Christian. Growing up, let's just say, between the two brothers, Sargon was the most responsible brother, and Christian, although he was known for his scientific achievements, he was also a renowned daredevil who always put himself in precarious situations. This one was no different. With his best friend George, they decided to travel far away to another forest for a hunting expedition near The Dark Forest. Riding along one afternoon, Christian stopped short. "George, do you hear something?"

They both came to a halt. "Like whispering?"

"Yes, like someone whispering 'help'."

"Yes, I hear something," agreed Christian as he spurred his horse towards the sound.

Forgetting about their hunting expedition, they followed the whispering deeper and deeper into The Dark Forest, towards The Black Forest.

"Christian, you know we're getting too close to The Black Forest, right? We shouldn't go any further."

"I know, George," responded Christian as they slowed to a walk.

"No one comes out of The Black Forest," stated George.

"George, I know, but that is where the sound is coming from. We must help whoever is in danger."

"I don't like it, but okay." They went further and deeper, and it got pretty dark.

"George, do you see that really faint glow up there?"

"No, I don't see anything. Wait…it's very, very faint. I almost missed it. Good eye Christian, but what is it?"

"I don't know, but listen…the closer we're getting, the whispering is getting louder. That must be it."

"I have an eerie feeling, and I don't like this one bit, Christian. We need to get out of here."

"Not till we see what that is." Christian's curiosity was growing stronger and there seemed to be something pulling him towards the glow.

As they got up to it, the whispering stopped, and there was dead silence. "George, keep an eye out."

"Okay, but hurry. We shouldn't be here. I have a bad feeling about this."

Christian dismounted his horse and looked under a partially rotted branch.

This is not possible, he thought to himself. He grabbed a leather pouch off his saddle and placed the rotted branch along with a debilitated turquoise flower inside.

"Ah Christian, there are a lot of red eyes popping up in the darkness. Now would be a really good time to leave."

As soon as Christian placed the flower and branch in the pouch, hissing and snarling rang out throughout the forest.

"This is bad Christian. They, whatever they are, obviously don't want us to take something out of their forest. We should hurry and get out of here now!"

"I'm with you, buddy. I can't believe what we've just found. We must leave this forest with it and our lives. Come on, we need to move George. Ride as fast as you can."

"You don't have to tell me twice. Let's go!" he cried, glancing back.

A dark mass was closing in on them. George was behind Christian, looking back at what appeared to be an angry mob of furry-legged creatures on their heels. "Christian, we've got company! What are those things? We're not going to make it!" cried George. The snarling and hissing were deafening.

"Keep going George, the forest's edge is just up there, hurry!" They were both whipping their horses, spurring them on.

"Faster!" Christian cried.

The creatures were hissing in unison, "Thieves! Bring that back! Get them!" Just as they were about to be engulfed by the creatures, the pouch carrying the flower flashed out a brilliant turquoise light, stopping the creatures in their tracks. Instantly, the nasty creatures screamed in agony and shrunk back into the darkness.

"What did they take?" hissed one of the Octospy. "My legs are burning from that flash."

"Mine too. I don't know exactly what that was, but we had better let our higher tier know what just happened. Nobody steals from us and makes it out alive."

"Keep going, George, hurry."

They rode like madmen back to The Ironwood Castle, getting themselves and the flower to safety.

"Did you see those things chasing us, Christian? I have never seen anything like that. No wonder no one goes into that forest. What was that flash of light?"

"I'm not sure, but whatever it was, it saved us big time. I have heard stories about creatures like that, George, but this is my first experience with them. Hopefully, my last."

"I don't understand how that flower survived in that wretched place or why such a flower would be in The Black Forest."

"You're kidding, right George? You don't recognize this flower?"

Christian recognized it immediately from bedtime stories his mother had read to him.

"No, I don't. What do you mean?"

"This flower is from The Lost Forest. We have made an incredibly important discovery, George! We must inform the King immediately. Only my brother must know about this. We need to get word to him… right away."

"Really… The Lost Forest? You are kidding, right? I've always thought that was a myth."

"A lot of people still think so. This flower only grew in The Lost Forest, according to ancient history and even bedtime stories my mother used to read to me. This flower must have sensed our presence and called out to us. Unreal."

"It is amazing that the flower survived all this time in that horrible atmosphere. What is truly unbelievable is that it wasn't discovered."

"You're right George. Unfortunately, its discovery is now known by the wrong factions. There will be severe backlash, I am sure of it."

"All the more reason to get it to safety. Let me pack my things and my horse, and I'll get word to King Sargon."

"Agreed, George. Reading my mind, my friend?"

George couldn't pack fast enough and was back down, ready to take off.

"Okay, Christian. It shouldn't take me too long to return to The Kingdom of the Meadow."

"Be careful, George. I will await the return of the King. I can't thank you enough."

"If you're right Christian, this is the biggest find of our lives. Nothing is more important now. I'll see you soon."

"See you soon," he responded as he rode off.

Christian went back inside the castle to tend to the precious flower and await his brother's arrival. The flash of light took its toll on the flower and branch, which were now almost disintegrated. "Let's see if I can remedy this situation," he thought to himself.

CHAPTER 14

The turquoise flower was now in the hands of King Sargon and his brother Christian, the Grand Duke. They were in seclusion at The Ironwood Castle, which was constructed long ago by an ancestor. The reclusive Duke of Ironwood desired privacy above all else, so he had searched diligently for an isolated location where he could be neither followed nor found. Upon finding the ideal place, he had a castle constructed from the largest and finest oak and ash trees in the forest. The long walls were so thick, they could never be penetrated, and so high, they could never be scaled. Upon completion of the castle, all those who had labored on its planning and construction, except for a few trusted confidants, were immediately and forever exiled to ensure that the location would never be divulged.

Entering the castle was impossible, for one was forced to navigate the most complex and unique maze walkway leading to the impressive front gates. While living, the reclusive Grand Duke refused to give another person the key to passing successfully through the maze. Thus, entrance was gained only by those in his company. He did possess the foresight to record the information that he held under lock and key to be opened only after his death. Thereafter, only two royals at a time were privy to this knowledge, which was verbally passed down through the generations. Little did the original Duke know that it would much later prove to be the ideal spot for his descendants to conceal the most important discovery of their lives – the key to saving The Lost Forest.

CHAPTER 15

"Christian! Where are you?"

"In here, Sargon," replied Christian. "Wow, you got here in record time!"

"This is hard to believe. Is it true? The flower, really?"

"Really Sargon. I can't believe it myself. We almost didn't make it out. If it weren't for the flower, we probably would be dead."

"George told me what happened. He said you guys were out hunting and heard this voice calling for help, so you ventured into The Black Forest following this voice, stupidly, I might add."

"I know it was stupid, brother, but it was drawing me in; I just couldn't fight the pull. The voice was too powerful. It was strange... I can't explain it."

"From the sounds of it, this flower saved you guys from being engulfed by the octospy. You guys are lucky to come out alive!"

"It was surreal, is all I can say. A brilliant flash of light stopped them in their tracks and let us get away."

Christian paused as he recalled the incident. "Anyway, it was clinging to this decayed branch when we discovered it. So, I scooped them up and headed back here. When I took the flower out of the pouch, the branch it was clinging to disintegrated into an unusual sparkling powder. That powder, I discovered, contained a high concentration of rare minerals. At the same time, the branch disintegrated, the flower wilted and secreted some sort of liquid. It was weird, but I got the feeling the two of them were trying to tell me something. It seemed to me the flower was clinging to the branch for dear life, like a lifeline. I decided to mix the liquid with the minerals and placed the flower's roots in the mixture, praying for its revival," explained Christian. "That seemed to be the ticket, Sargon," Christian went on. "Not only did the flower flourish, but somehow the branch reformed and has reattached itself to the flower, or vice versa."

"Very intriguing. A natural symbiotic relationship," Sargon surmised.

"Yes," replied Christian, "it seems that the branch saved her, and she saved the branch."

"To me, it looks like you saved them both. Had you not thought of mixing its secretion with the branch's remnants, they both may have died. Look how beautiful she is. The turquoise color is quite intense, I must say, and that branch looks like the same wood as our castle. Strong," stressed Sargon.

"One more thing that is quite interesting," Christian added.

"What's that, brother?" Sargon asked.

Christian extended his hand toward the flower, and the flower leaned into Christian's hand as part of her vine wrapped around his wrist. Gently stroking one of the petals with his thumb, Christian then withdrew his hand from her.

"That's quite fascinating," Sargon exclaimed. "How did you discover that?"

"This morning, early, I came in to see what kind of progress she was making and was so happy to see her rehydrated and looking good. I went to touch one of her petals, and the same thing you just saw happened."

"If I didn't know any better, Christian, I think she knows you saved her."

"It seems so, doesn't it?" smirked Christian.

"Is the flower in good enough condition to travel?" inquired Sargon.

"Aren't we waiting for Victoria?" asked Christian.

"She was adamant that if she got held up, I was to go on and she would catch up. I wasn't happy about it, but she was right. This discovery will save all of us and we must safeguard it at all costs. I am surprised, however, that she hasn't arrived. I hope she hasn't run into trouble. I know she is quite capable of handling herself, but she should have been here by now. It's worrisome," said Sargon.

"She is not one to be reckoned with, I dare say, but she is with her guard, right?" Christian asked.

"She is," Sargon replied. "The sooner we get this flower to the Prince's Kingdom, the better. She would do the same. I hate not waiting for her, but we can't risk the flower being discovered. You know she wouldn't wait for me Christian." The King smirked at his brother.

Christian chuckled at his brother and responded, "She would have already left by now, whether you were on time or not. Anyways, Sargon, I think Cleo, as I named her, is looking good enough for travel.

I just need a little time to construct a carrier, both for her safety and her secrecy. What do you say, Sargon, first thing in the morning?"

"Yes. I'll get us ready for our journey."

"Sargon, does Prince Talus know we are coming?"

"No, he does not. We are the only ones besides Victoria who know of this flower. The fewer people that know about our flower, the better off we are right now."

"I must say, I am curious to see the Prince's kingdom. I know you were there a while ago with father, so you know he is not a myth. But he remains a myth around the forests. Are you sure he exists?" Christian asked jokingly.

"Just wait, Christian. His kingdom is like nothing you will have or ever see."

"Clever, Sargon, very clever."

"In all seriousness though," Sargon continued, "the Prince's family has been invaluable in helping a lot of very important individuals disappear, all without being seen. Being a chameleon obviously helps. He and his family's kingdom are very well-hidden, hence his reputation of being a myth. Need I say more? We are never to speak of him on our journey as you never know who might be listening."

"Of course. Like I said Sargon, looking forward to it."

"I'll get us ready while you take care of Cleo and company. Good night, Christian."

"Good night, brother."

CHAPTER 16

Still hunkering down at Keewae's, the following morning, they gathered again. "If I may, Victoria, how was Shift able to get to Nia?" asked Chuck.

"She was kidnapped right under our noses one night, shortly after these two were born," looking over at Salair. "We found one nanny unconscious and tied up in a closet. Someone obviously dressed up as a nanny and stole Nia. It must have been Shift's wife. That would explain a lot. We searched everywhere but to no avail. I became so paranoid that Salair would be stolen that we asked Sasha to be by her side 24/7. Shift and his wife no doubt took good care of her, which I should be grateful for, but I will never forgive them for what they did."

"Shift did tell us that Drouck killed his wife and stole Nia," explained Chuck. "Unfortunately, I wish we had asked him more detailed questions about Nia, but we had no idea, Your Highness," he went on.

"Thank you, Chuck, but you had no idea," responded the Queen. "Shift's wife couldn't be a rat. There is no way she would have gotten past the guards," the Queen continued. "I don't know how we are going to find Nia now. Hopefully, they left a trail I can track. The longer we wait, the less chance we have of saving her. I cannot go any further without her. I won't lose her again." The Queen was livid. Everyone was stunned.

"We'll never stop until we find her," continued Sasha, "now we know she is alive."

"That is the good news, Your Highness," said Kehi.

"Yes," the Queen agreed and looked up. "Yes, yes, it is good news."

"We'll get her back, Your Highness. I am sorry, I didn't pursue them further."

"You didn't have any clue Kehi, and we were in no position to chase after them. We couldn't have taken the chance or else all of us would have been imprisoned. Shift will be hunted down, and he will pay for what he has done to our family," the Queen stated with resolve.

CHAPTER 17

"Dad," cried Nia. "Slow down." She was out of breath and couldn't figure out why he was in such a hurry. She could see that he was panicking.

"We can't slow down," Shift replied. "We must get out of this forest as soon as possible." Shift added as he grabbed her arm and yanked her forward.

"Ouch, Daddy, you're hurting me. What is wrong with you?" Nia said in an annoyed tone and pulled her arm away from him. "Why aren't we waiting for the others? Why did you grab me away from the Queen? Do you know the Queen? She seemed so familiar to me."

Shift was frantic with fear. He knew the Queen would send pursuers now that she had recognized Nia. "You out of your mind? How would we know the Queen? Just because you spent a week with her doesn't make you familiar with her."

"No, Dad, that's not it. I felt something familiar when she held my hand. Like I know her somehow. There was an instant connection – that feeling is something I can't explain."

"Trust me! I am telling you, Nia, you don't know her. Don't be a fool. I came back to rescue you from Drouck, and you question me about some prisoner of Drouck's? Ungrateful wretch. If we get caught again, we are both dead. Now let's go," he snarled.

"You are calling me an ungrateful wretch? After what I have been through... after mother was killed? How dare you say that to me. Locked up in a castle with a deranged person, fearing for my life? Why did you tear me away from the Queen? You know something. I have a bad feeling you are not telling me the truth," Nia said, agitated.

"How dare you question me? I'm not answerable to you. If you want to get out of here, you better come with me." Shift was glaring at her now. "Let's go. Now!" Shift stared at her. Nia knew he was lying to her by the look in his eyes.

Noticing Shift's reactions, Nia decided to go along and get out of the forest to get away from him. The glimpses of recent events started flashing through her mind: the haste at leaving the others at the castle, her feeling of familiarity with the Queen, the Queen's anguish when Shift rushed her away, and now, her father's rash, inexplicable actions assured her that there was something Shift was hiding something from her.

"Dad, am I related to the Queen?" she blurted out.

"Don't be stupid!" snarling at her. "How could you be?"

"I don't know, but when she held my hand and I looked into her eyes, I felt like we knew each other."

"Like I said, you don't! How could you?" He laughed at her. It was a cruel, mocking laugh.

"How... indeed?" she thought, again troubled by his reaction. "I knew her, and she knew me," she thought to herself quietly. Especially after the ends of their hair mysteriously illuminated, which, until she met the Queen, had never happened before. She wasn't even going to mention that part. She remained quiet as she followed her father, blinking back tears now. She knew she couldn't get out of this part of the forest and away from Drouck without him.

Nia was told by her 'parents' that they found her as a baby – abandoned in a remote part of the forest and had mercifully taken her to their home, loved her, and cared for her as their own. Indeed, she had been content with that explanation until now. However, she had questions now. 'Who am I? Who would have abandoned me? Why? Where did I come from? Why did I feel so irresistibly drawn to the Queen? Why did she seem to know me'? Dad, or whoever he is, she decided, is acting too defensive about my questions. Nia had a bad feeling now, especially judging from Shift's reaction to her questions. "I must get away from Shift at the first opportunity I get and go find the Queen," she thought.

CHAPTER 18

"So sorry to interrupt," Corga excused while entering the room. "Sir Charles, I was going to change Sleet's bandage and check on him. I assume you would like to accompany me?"

"Why thank you, Corga, you read my mind. Excuse me, your Majesty."

"Of course, Chuck. I hope you find Sleet well."

With Berra perched on his shoulder, they went up to check on his injured stallion. Upon arriving upstairs, they found all the horses sleeping except for Sleet. He was awake and looked peaceful. Berra flew off Sir Charles' shoulder, landed right next to Sleet, and sang a peaceful note. Sleet bowed his head in understanding.

"How's my boy?" Chuck said as he came over and stroked his silky nose, feeling great relief.

"Wow!" exclaimed Corga. "He looks amazing, considering the amount of poison he had in his system."

"Don't underestimate these horses, Corga. They are true warriors."

"Yes indeed, Sir," Corga agreed and knelt at Sleet's injured ankle. "Let's change this bandage, Sleet." He then unwound the bandage. "This looks good, but there is still a spot down here I don't like. One more extraction, Sir Charles. This shouldn't be too painful."

Chuck held Sleet's face, "Okay boy, one more time."

Corga used a smaller needle this time, and Sleet only groaned slightly. "Great," Corga said with a smile. "A little more salve, and I'll put a fresh wrap on it. Sir Charles, this looks good. Sleet, you are amazing," said Corga, stroking the animal's glistening neck.

"They all are, Corga," Sir Charles replied, his eyes roving over the other magnificent stallions, then back to Corga. "I can't thank you enough. I know very well you saved his life."

"Thank you. I will get him some oats to eat with the naida. He needs to build some strength back up."

"Right behind you, brother." Sin Sin came in with a big bucket of just that and some water.

Chuck just watched in admiration while they fed and watered his horses. "Impressive young fuzzars," he thought to himself. "All right, boy. You eat up and get your strength back. We're going to need you shortly," he said while stroking Sleet's head. Sleet nudged Chuck back.

Downstairs, Salair was staring at her mother, admiring her will. "Mother, you must be exhausted. I don't know how you did it all these years without Nia."

"I had no choice. You must carry on no matter how painful things get. I still had you to love and protect. But I must admit that not knowing whatever happened to your sister has been torturous for your father and I."

"I can't believe how all this turned out to be."

"What do you mean?"

"Well, Shift just happens to find Sir Charles when we showed up at his castle. Then he leads us to his supposed 'daughter', finding you and Nia in the same place at the same time."

"I've always believed things work out for a reason. It was meant to be. We will find her, no matter what it takes. Shift will be hunted down. I can promise you that." Victoria stared at Salair with a hardened look she'd never seen before.

Trying to lighten the situation, she chimed in, "I can't imagine life without her anymore, mother." She squeezed her hand. Victoria softened her look and stroked her daughter's hair. "Me neither, Salair."

"If you don't mind, I'm going upstairs to see how the horses are doing."

"And Chuck?"

"Mostly the horses, mother. Don't be silly."

Victoria knew better. Since she was very young, every time Sir Charles trained with her husband, Salair was always hiding somewhere to watch the young warrior. She just smiled at her daughter. "See you in a minute then."

Salair had Corga take her upstairs to check on Chuck and the horses. "Chuck, is everything okay? How's Sleet doing?"

"Salair," Chuck smiled appreciatively at her. "He is going to be just fine. Corga and Sin Sin are miracle workers. I don't think he would have survived without them."

"Yes, all these little fuzzars are very impressive."

"How's your mother doing?"

"After what she has been through…her strength and determination is admirable. Obviously, finding Nia alive is something she probably could never have imagined. I think that has given her renewed strength. We must find her, Chuck. I know you will do everything in your power to help find her."

"No stone unturned, Salair. No matter what it takes."

"It is astounding, you know."

"What's that, Salair?"

"The discovery of the turquoise flower and then being led to Nia by her own kidnapper? Truly a miracle."

"The past series of events is nothing short of astounding," said Chuck.

Meanwhile, Kehi was visiting with the Queen.

"Kehi?" addressed the Queen.

"Yes, Your Highness?"

"How are your tracking skills?" she inquired. Kehi knew at once why she asked him that.

"I am quite skilled, Your Highness," he replied quietly. "Why do you ask?"

"I know you are unaware of my past, Kehi, but before I met the King, I was a great huntress in my own right. Thanks to my father."

She had his rapt attention. "How is that, Your Highness?"

"My father was a world-renowned hunter and marksman. He also had degrees in chemistry and botany. He taught me everything he knew. He spent years teaching me how to track any kind of insect or animal. He had me study different kinds of soil from all the various forests we are privy to, and finally, he taught me how to fight, using all kinds of weaponry. But his greatest interest was the mud that protects the fuzzars."

"How so?" inquired Kehi.

"My mother was killed by that mud."

"That is horrible, Your Highness. So sorry to hear that," said Kehi.

"Thank you. My father was devastated. He never forgave himself. He became obsessed with analyzing and studying this mud and stayed up at all hours, day and night. It was sad and exhausting watching him. One day, he said he was going out for a few supplies. Before he left, he gave me a big hug, took my hand, and told me he loved me. I thought it was a bit strange at the time because he was just going to get supplies. I never saw him again. To this day, I am not sure if he is dead or alive." The Queen looked away from Kehi for a moment. He kept silent. The Queen went on, "After he didn't come back, I packed up all his meticulous writings of his works over the years and, upon doing so, ran across his notes and drawings on the mud that killed my mother. He never shared this information with me – too painful, I guess. But, according to his notes, this mud is quite complex, like it's its own organism. I must not say any more, I'm sorry. I've probably said too much already."

"If I may, Your Highness, where are all these notes? Wouldn't something like that be highly secretive?"

"Yes, they would be. They are locked away in our castle, and no one but me and the King is privy to their whereabouts.

"I am sorry for such a loss of your family. First, your parents and then Nia disappearing. Your strength is admirable," revered Kehi as he tried to change the subject because this news made him a little uncomfortable.

"When I realized my father was not coming back, it was agony all over again. First my mother and then him. But I knew I had to go on," added the Queen.

"I haven't shared a lot of my past with Salair, and I really don't know why I am telling you this, but I feel I can trust you."

"Without a doubt, Your Highness," replied Kehi.

"Thank you, Kehi. On that note, I would like you and I to go back to Drouck's camp and track Nia from there. I won't take another step away from this forest until we find her. If I have to go alone, I will and am perfectly capable. I can't order you to go with me, but I would strongly ask it as a favor."

Kehi replied, "I thought you would never ask. I have been beating myself up for not being able to catch them the first time. However, you know Salair will not like this one bit."

"Like what?" Salair inquired as she re-entered the room along with Chuck.

"It seems your mother has recruited me on a new mission."

"Oshiro, what is it?" asked Chuck.

"Her Majesty has asked me to help her track and find Nia," Kehi replied.

"Mother!" cried Salair, "that is insane. Do you know what you are saying and doing? That is out of the question. Besides, you are still recovering. I don't want to hear anything about it."

"Stop... right now!" snapped the Queen. "This is my decision and mine alone. Like I told Kehi, I will not leave this forest until I find your sister. I won't lose her again. You may not like it, Salair, but I will do everything in my power to find Nia. And that's final."

"I don't know what to say, Your Highness," interrupted Chuck. "It just seems awfully dangerous to just let the two of you go off into this dangerous forest. Kehi is a skilled tracker, but... "

At that moment, Kehi interrupted, "Apparently, her Highness is a skilled tracker, amongst other things... from her youth, she tells me."

"Really, mother. I guess there is a lot I apparently don't know about you, and you have not told me." Salair was miffed, to say the least. The Queen looked at Salair.

"It's a lot for you right now. I get it," Victoria said. "I understand I haven't shared a lot of things with you. With all my duties as Queen, I'm afraid our relationship has suffered. I promise I will make it up to you, Salair. Please forgive me." Salair looked up at the Queen and nodded with a forgiving smile.

"I can't stop you, Your Highness," interrupted Keewae, "but you must realize how dangerous this forest is. It would be a fool's errand."

"I understand how you feel, Keewae, but you must understand how I feel – all of you must understand this. I won't leave her behind. I will find her. My father taught me well. I have no doubt that Kehi will be a great protector and provide invaluable help." Kehi nodded in affirmation.

"Well, I guess that's it!" Sir Charles yielded, aware the Queen would not be talked out of it.

"We meet in the morning for a plan, I assume," said Victoria. "Ready, Salair?" It was a politely worded command.

Keewae waited until they were out of earshot, heaving a sigh of relief and exclaiming, "Wow, the Queen has the determination of an avalanche."

"She is a warrior. I admire that," stated Chuck. "Oshi," Chuck said jokingly, "are you going to be able to keep up with her?"

"I'm just glad we are on the same side," he said.

Keewae got serious. "You know it's going to be unbelievably dangerous out there?"

"I do, but I feel between the two of us, it will be okay. I don't know how to explain it," said Kehi.

"I know what you mean, Oshi," said Chuck.

"There is something strong and mysterious about her, Keewae. You will be instrumental in a plan for them, of course."

"I know. Let's get some rest and meet in the morning. This has been an unbelievable day."

CHAPTER 19

Nia followed behind Shift, trying to come up with some plan. Shift was sure now that Nia knew something, but not even close to everything. He had to lead her as far away from Drouck's camp and the Queen as possible. He knew the Queen would have him killed if they found him. Drouck knows where Shift lives, so there was danger at both ends.

"Dad!" cried Nia. "Where are we going? Back to the house?"

"No, Nia. We can never go back there," snapped Shift. "Drouck knows by now that his prisoner was taken, and you're gone too. He'll be out of his mind. He knows where we live, and he'll send his men out to find you and take you back."

"What are we going to do then?" Nia asked, panicked.

"I don't know. We can't stop here. Keep going." He yanked her arm forward. "I'll figure something out," he grumbled.

Nia was in full panic mode now. Shift didn't have a plan, and she didn't want to be stuck with him anymore. She was convinced more than ever that she had to find the Queen. She decided to play along with Shift until she had an opening to escape him.

"I guess we have to go back to the house, but just to get our things and go from there," Shift told Nia, finally breaking the silence.

"All right, dad," she replied quietly.

"Keep your eyes open for Drouck's men," he said. "I am sure they will search for the Queen before they come after you, but you just don't know with Drouck," Shift went on. Nia remained quiet but wary of her surroundings. She knew Shift wouldn't hurt her, but she wanted to get away from him. He wasn't her father, and her mother was dead, who probably wasn't her mother either. She was devastated and confused. Nia needed to know the truth, and it wasn't going to come from Shift.

CHAPTER 20

The next morning, they all gathered again. "I must reiterate how secretive this find must remain," expressed Queen Victoria. "There are only four people right now that know about this."

"Sorry, Your Highness, but whoever got word to you about the flower had to know as well?" Chuck asked.

"The information was brought to him by his brother's trusted friend, who was there when they made the discovery. Betrayal wouldn't have crossed his mind," she added.

"After the King got word of the find, he headed out immediately, knowing I would be safe at the castle without him."

"I am perplexed how you were even kidnapped, Your Majesty. The castle is highly secure," stated Chuck.

"That has been bothering me as well. Sargon and Sasha have gone to great lengths to find the right men. He would have never left me alone if he thought there was a problem. We didn't travel together for obvious reasons."

"Of course, Your Highness. Having the two of you captured would be the end of the kingdom," replied Chuck.

"Exactly," replied Victoria. "The day I was captured, I was upstairs packing and didn't hear anyone come in the room. The next thing I remember was waking up in that awful cage with Drouck. I am guessing we must have foiled Drouck's plan."

"Why do you say that mother?"

"Well, obviously, he was expecting both of us. He was furious that the two of us weren't captured. He took his anger out on his men and me. I wasn't about to tell him anything and he was well aware of it. He hit me anyway. I would have died before telling him anything. I'm just thankful you came along when you did."

"Yes, very thankful!" exclaimed Salair. "What a coward he is. The whole thing makes me sick."

"There is still a problem at the castle," remarked Kehi. "That should have never happened. Sounds to me like there may be a mole in the ranks."

"That would make more sense!" said the Queen.

"Well, that doesn't bode well for going back to the castle until we figure out who this person is," said Sasha.

"I say we head back to my fortress for safety reasons and head operations there," suggested Chuck. "Keewae, without divulging the information about the flower, can your underground network get information through to the King and his brother that we are heading to Sir Charles' fortress? The whereabout of his fortress is already known to the King."

Keewae summoned the little fuzzars for their intake. "Corga," said Keewae, "this is the most important information we will ever send out. There can absolutely be no leaks about the whereabouts of the King's fortress. It would be death to all of us if this information got into the wrong hands. I trust you know the messenger I am talking about?"

Corga stared at Keewae for a minute, and then he got it. "Perfect choice Uncle. If you will excuse me, I must locate this asset."

"If you will, Your Majesty, this way to our 'workshop'. We can work on your message and get it to the King's location," said Sin Sin.

"Of course," said the Queen, "after you."

"I keep saying it Keewae, those three are impressive," admired Chuck. "How did this underground come about anyway?" inquired Kehi.

"After their mother died, the three of them were so distraught that they withdrew from activities and stayed in touch with their friends. However, their friends wouldn't let their depression get them down, so they started sending them notes once a week telling them how they missed them and what was going on in the forest. That seemed to brighten and intrigue their spirits, which, in turn, helped them recover from their sadness. It just blossomed from there – so much so that the fuzzars became the central command, if you will. There was so much trust in the passing of their information that it was decided to put them in charge of receiving and sending information about the happenings in the forest. Many creatures were saved. The forest will never change, though. It will always be very dangerous," explained Keewae.

"So, in a way, a silent spy network?" inquired Kehi.

"Of sorts, yes, Kehi!" He went on, "I think the Queen will appreciate our secretive and trustworthy network."

"I find the timing of the discovery of this flower quite intriguing," said Kehi.

"How so?"

Kehi continued, "More and more forests are going dark. It's not just Prince Drouck and his army that are growing and slowly encroaching on other forests. His friend, Octimus, likewise is on the march, creating even more destructive octospies that, in turn, are destroying even more forests. They must be stopped at all costs."

"Ah yes. I get where you are going, Kehi."

"Are you saying this flower knows something we don't, Kehi?" asked Chuck.

"I cannot pretend to even know this flower, but in ancient times, my ancestors used certain flower species to ward off evil. How they did it... Well, there is an ancient written key that was lost a long time ago. I wouldn't be surprised if this flower has the same powers and is sensing exactly what is happening. This flower must get to safety."

"I like my protective surroundings and my family, but I agree Chuck, we must restore the goodness we once enjoyed," responded Keewae.

CHAPTER 21

"How's it going, Christian?" asked the King, "About ready, brother?"

"Yes, I'll meet you out front. I've got our flower and branch safely housed in her carrier, as you can see. Sargon, why are we taking Cleo to Prince Talus? Does he know anything about this flower?"

"I don't know the answer to that. What I do know is that we're heading to his palace for two reasons. First, for protection, and second, he is the only one of two families who holds ancient secrets about the forests in our land."

"Do you know who the other family is?"

"I shouldn't say it's a family per se; it's a powerful fairy, the Rose Fairy. Father told me about her a long time ago. He said their ties were historical, but he never got around to explaining what those were. The fact that you found Cleo – no offense, brother, but I believe Cleo found you – is, according to the myth, the beginning of her quest to restore The Lost Forest."

Christian didn't reply but simply stared quizzically at his elder brother.

"Don't look so perplexed, little brother. I say that, remembering the condition she was in when you found her. In all that darkness, she sensed goodness coming her way and was willing to die to call for help. All the more reason I want to get us to the Prince."

"Understood, Sargon. We're ready." They saddled up, Cleo in hand, and headed down the maze away from their fortress. As they rounded the last part of the maze, the horses stopped suddenly, ears perking up.

"What is it?" whispered Christian while stroking his horse to comfort him. He glanced over at Sargon, who placed his finger over his lips. They waited quietly. Sargon dismounted and walked to the end of the maze. A deer ran through the forest about fifty yards away from him.

"It was just a deer," said Sargon. They set out again.

"Something is wrong," said Christian. "The horses are on edge." Before his brother could answer, a huge red spider launched itself at Christian, sweeping him off his horse.

"Christian!" yelled the King, frantically flying off his horse and yanking his sword from its scabbard as he raced toward the gigantic spider attacking his brother. Before Sargon could get to Christian, the spider was entwined by a leafy vine that squeezed the life from it. When the vine relaxed its grip on the now-dead spider, a turquoise flash sliced through the forest, making sure no others would follow. Christian shoved the spider off, but in so doing, his hands got burned from touching the red creature.

"Ahh!" he screamed from the pain, "my hands!" They began to blister and turn black.

"Oh no, Christian!" yelled Sargon as they both stared in horror at his hands. "Let me get something to wrap your hands in." As he started to run back to his horse, Cleo beat him to it, dropping a flower petal on each hand. In turn, the petals melded against his skin, pulling out the venomous poison. His blisters began to dissipate. Christian just stood there holding his hands out in disbelief and relief. The pain and blisters were gone and they both stared in amazement as the vine recoiled itself back into the carrier that Christian had constructed.

Christian looked at the King and almost whispered, "Can you believe that?"

"No, I cannot. How are your hands?" He was just as stunned as his little brother.

"Like nothing ever happened," He replied, holding them up in amazement. Christian looked into the carrier, his eyes wide with amazement at Cleo.

"Let's get out of here," said Sargon, watching Cleo in awe. "We can ill afford to hang around here. Little did they know that the flash of light Cleo sent out was a message to The Dark Forest."

"Looks like we have a new protector, Sargon," Christian stated as he remounted his horse.

"It appears so," agreed the bewildered King. He spurred his horse into a swift canter.

"Wait!" said Christian as he shored up alongside his brother. "Do you see that, brother?" he asked.

"I do, although it's very faint," replied Sargon, noticing a very faint turquoise trail before them.

"What do you make of that?"

"Well, seeing how the trail is leading in that direction, it means that somehow Cleo knows the way to the Kingdom."

"Coincidence... you think?" asked Christian.

"I dare say no, Christian. Let's follow the trail but with great caution. Not that I don't trust Cleo, but this is getting a little hard to fathom."

Christian looked behind them and was shocked all over again, "Hey, look behind us, Sargon."

The King turned and observed only the usual pathway. The turquoise glow was not in evidence anywhere behind them. "Talk about covering your tracks," he muttered quietly, then calling to his brother, he said, "Stay on alert, Christian. We still need to protect Cleo, although I am beginning to think it is the other way around."

"That's the second time she has saved me. First with George and now with you. Incredible!"

As they went on their journey, every so often, Cleo touched the ground with her extended vines and flashed the turquoise trail, leading them to the Kingdom of the Chameleons.

CHAPTER 22

Once the Queen went back to the office with the young fuzzars to give them instructions meant for the King, she noticed that the office walls were not solid mud like the rest of the house. Instead, they were interwoven with the same type of vines that captured them when they first arrived.

"That will make it much easier to get through," she thought to herself while staring at the wall.

"My Queen?"

"Ah yes, Corga," she replied, interrupting her thoughts. The Queen drafted her message and handed it to Corga.

"Here you go, my dear. I'll leave you to your work then. God's speed to your courier. Thank you for your help. It is so much appreciated."

"Of course, Your Majesty. Anything we can do for the Kingdom."

Not returning to the others, the Queen slipped back to her room and packed the items she would need on her journey. A few pieces of the fuzzars' special porcelain for a weapon were also placed in her bag.

She wrote out a note for Salair and waited for the fuzzars to come out of 'the office'. Everyone was still in the main room and busy with discussions when Corga and Sin Sin returned.

"We're all set with the Queen," Sin Sin announced, emerging from the back.

"Great," said Keewae, "I hope it doesn't take too long to get word to the King."

"We are taking extra precautions this time, Uncle," chimed in Corga. "We don't want to take any chances with this priceless information."

While the little fuzzars were busy updating their Uncle about their preparations, the Queen sneakily slipped back to the office. She stood there a moment, studying the wall, and picked her spot. She looked around to make sure no one was coming and wound around through the mud precisely as her father had taught her. Outside, Queen Victoria glanced around one more time to ensure no one had observed her escape. She then dove through the leafy wall where they came in and headed back to Drouck's camp.

"Sorry, Kehi," the Queen whispered under her breath. She didn't want to put anyone else in danger and take extra protection away from Salair.

"Is my mother still back there?" asked Salair.

"No, she left our office. I thought she came out here," said Corga.

"Well, maybe she went to rest for a bit. I'll go check on her," said Salair. "Mother? Are you back here?" Salair looked around the room and noticed a note on the bed. "What is this?" Picking up the piece of paper, she screamed, "Oh my god! No!"

Salair went running back out to everyone, shouting, "My mother is not in her room!" Waving the note in her hand, disbelief on her face. "She's gone!"

They all jumped to their feet.

"She left me this," she said, handing the note to Chuck, who began reading.

My Dearest Salair,

I am going to find your sister. I will not return home without her. Go on without me. Nia and I will join you at Sir Charles' fortress. I have decided against taking Kehi. He is needed here with you. No one is to try to follow me. They would not be able to.

I love you very much,

Mother.

"Whoa!" exclaimed Chuck after reading the letter aloud and reaching for the teary-eyed Princess, who buried her face in Chuck's chest.

"Nantekotta!" exhaled Kehi as he took the note from his friend's hand and read it for himself.

"What?" Keewae was mystified. "I... she isn't back there? There is no exit or other way out of that room."

"Corga," said Keewae, "tell us what happened. Did the Queen send the message and then come out?"

"Yes, Uncle. She left her instructions with us and then excused herself. I assumed she was going to join everyone. We then went to work getting the instructions to our messenger. Apparently, she went to her room and left the note for Salair. From there Uncle, I have no idea. I am so sorry. I don't know what to say." Corga seemed visibly upset.

"That's exactly what happened, Uncle. This is terrible!" stated Sin Sin.

Keewae came over and hugged them both. "It's not your fault. You had no idea."

"Don't you dare blame yourselves," scolded Salair. "This has nothing to do with you. My mother disappeared on her own. But where? Could she get out of here, Keewae?"

"There was one thing, Uncle. I don't know if it means anything, but when we went back to the office, she was staring at the wall behind us."

"What do you mean, staring?" inquired Keewae.

"Yes, that's right," said Sin Sin. "Like she was studying it."

"I'm not sure what that could mean," said Keewae. "There is no way to get out of here without one of us, as you all know." Keewae said, "Alright you three, it's time to check the house."

The looks on their faces were quite evident. Check the house means for them to go up top, check the surroundings, and kill any enemy they see. Keewae had taught them that a long time ago. They have not had to deal with that since living with their Uncle. They are still fuzzars, after all, and very dangerous.

"Yes, Uncle," they said as they separated.

"Keewae, what can we do?" questioned Chuck.

"Nothing, as you know, no one can leave here without one of us. I am very perplexed right now. This makes no sense. There is no way she could have left, and if she did, I am sorry, but as we told you when you got here, no one would survive that mud," explained Keewae.

"That may not be entirely true, Keewae," said Kehi.

"I think I would know, Kehi," objected Keewae. "This mud is foolproof protection," he went on.

"Why do you say that Kehi?" asked Salair.

"Did you know your mother was an expert on soil? She told me about her past with her father. Her mother was killed by this same mud. In short, her father spent countless hours analyzing and studying the properties of the mud. She didn't really say if he discovered what made up the properties, but I have a feeling she knew something about it... No offense, Keewae," elucidated Kehi. He didn't want to go too far, as he gave the Queen his word.

"I had no idea," said Salair. "So, there could be a chance that she is alive?"

"I don't want to give false hope, but she is very resourceful and mysterious, I might add, Salair. I wouldn't discount her for a second." Kehi went on.

"Well, that would be a first for my family if she was able to get through my walls without anything happening," grumbled Keewae.

"For our sake, we should assume that she did get through, and I'll bet you ten to one she is headed back to Drouck's camp," said Chuck.

"Well, we must stick to the plan like we discussed with the Queen," said Kehi. "No offense, Salair, but if she is alive, she would want us to get to the flower and the King first."

"None taken, Kehi. You are right! My mother would not be happy if we tried to follow her, as much as it pains me to think about her alone in this nasty place."

"Just remember, Salair, your mother is a warrior. From what she was telling me, she can handle herself pretty well."

"I will have my nephews put the word out about your mother and get any information they can find back to us, Princess," offered Keewae in a comforting tone. "We have certain denizens that are the highest tier of information gatherers that Corga will put on tracking your mother. I can't promise much, but if anyone can find out anything, they are the ones."

"Please do. Anything would be welcome," sighed the Princess.

"Not to be callous, Princess, we need to refocus our efforts and prepare to get across The Magic Forest," said Keewae.

"I understand. There is nothing we can do right now. I can't believe my mother would do this. She won't quit until she finds my sister if she is indeed still alive."

"How long do you think it will take us to get through the forest?" asked Chuck.

"It could take a while; the forest is very tricky and dangerous. I am sorry to be vague, Chuck, but it is nothing like you have ever seen or been through."

Chuck doubted that, thinking of the many precarious situations he had survived, but said, "My horses will be of help. Berra, of course, will fly overhead and scout for us."

"Berra will help, and your Arabians can be an asset, but they could be more of a liability. They will alleviate a great deal of walking, but the path we are taking is very treacherous.

Chuck was determined to take his beloved stallions, so he outlined his reasoning, "On foot, it will take days. My horses will save us precious time. They will be useful in countless other situations, also."

"The forest is dangerous, and taking them may add a troublesome dimension to the trip," Keewae asserted.

Chuck was acutely aware that Keewae was extremely reluctant to take his unique animals, so he pressed Keewae a bit further, "I understand what you are saying, Keewae, but these horses are born protectors. Their hooves are razor sharp, they are much stronger than the average horse, have a great deal more stamina, and run as fast as a cheetah." He continued talking, relating how they had saved his life many times in past battles and some of the trials the horses had endured.

"I understand," said Keewae, finally willing to concede and apparently convinced by the lengthy argument that Chuck had just presented. "It sounds as if they are exactly what we need. I will incorporate them into our trip. If you will excuse me, I need to grab my maps and prepare for our trip. I bet everyone is tired and should get their rest, as I am sure this trip will be anything but restful."

They all nodded in agreement and headed to their respective rooms, except Salair. Chuck circled back when he saw her sitting there.

"Princess, I know your mother is still alive, and as Keewae said, he will have his nephews update us on her progress. They have a very sophisticated network. I have no doubt they will find her," he reassured, squeezing her hand.

"I feel like she is okay. She never really talked about herself. She's always busy with father running our kingdom. We never seem to have any time to spend with each other. Maybe... I can change that when this comes to an end." Salair squeezed Chuck's hand back.

"You'll have a lot of catching up to do with her and your new-found sister."

"I am hopeful I will get to meet her," she replied as she stood up. "I guess we better try to get some rest. We have quite the journey ahead of us, it seems," she added while holding Chuck's hand and looking into his eyes.

CHAPTER 23

Queen Victoria had no trouble backtracking to Drouck's castle and made it to the edge of the forest, where Sleet was attacked by the giant spider. It sent chills up her spine, but she was not to be deterred. She was enraged with Shift stealing her precious Nia, and that steeled her nerves, making her forget about the dangers ahead of her. Victoria decided her best bet was to stay off the ground as much as possible. She figured she would be better protected in the trees, and as brainless as most of Drouck's men were, they would not be looking up to find anyone anyway, and she would be away from anything deadly on the ground. "Hurry up, it's getting dark," she thought to herself.

"My Queen, a long way from home, aren't we?"

"What, who said that?" She scanned the big trees in front of her. "And you are?" she asked as her eyes settled on a particular tree that looked very similar to the one in front of their main castle.

"I'm Cottonwood's descendant, my Queen!" The regal tree bowed slightly.

"Cottonwood? I must say I'm impressed. And you are? What are you doing in this part of the forest?"

"I go by 'Raspin', Your Highness. Cottonwood's seeds spread wide and far in every part of the forests, and our services are called upon from time to time. It seems we were summoned by the great one once something was found... if you know what I mean."

"Yes, I do," she replied in a serious tone.

"He has summoned a great number of us in every direction. Additionally, your disappearance was very alarming to Cottonwood. Unfortunately, we did not sprout in time to help you and the others out of the forest the first time."

"I am dumbfounded by this information. I had no idea Cottonwood reigned over the trees of the land." Cottonwood is the largest tree in The Kingdom of the Meadow and is centuries old.

"It's been a protected secret for centuries. With the recent discovery, Cottonwood will be getting more aggressive about sending us into precarious situations. That is why Cottonwood is now summoning us. I am sure he meant no disrespect to the Kingdom. We have been sent to get you to your daughter and get you both out."

"That's incredible, Raspin. I understand. Thank you for being here."

"My Queen, it is getting dark, and you must get off the ground. If I may?"

"Yes, of course."

Raspin lowered his mighty branch, and the Queen climbed on board.

"My Queen, we will be here when you get Nia out, but it must be quick. Popping up in this nasty forest puts us at risk, and Cottonwood only allows us to stay a certain amount of time, and then we are gone. That is what has kept our secret and us safe all these years."

"Understood. Time is of the essence."

Raspin's tree army formed a walkway that allowed the Queen safe passage across the forest and to the edge of the clearing. She took a quick look around the grounds. "It is unusually quiet," she thought. There was a faint glow coming from one side of the castle, but she also noticed that red eyes were staring at her from the edge of the clearing where she had just come from. "Yes, I see you. I'll be gone before you know it, wretched creatures," she whispered under her breath. Let's see what is going on in there." She took off and ran through the servant quarters door since she was familiar with that part of the castle. The servants seemed to be in for the night, so she didn't have to worry about running into any of them. She peered out the door and looked down at the faintly lit hallway. She made her way down the hallway towards the section that was lit up. The Queen stopped short of rounding the corner as she could hear voices coming from the room just up ahead of her. Then her mouth fell open as she whispered 'Nia' in disbelief.

"I told you, I had no choice, Your Highness. Shift just grabbed me and pulled me through the forest."

"I don't believe you, Nia. You are a liar. Who let the Queen out and killed my men!" screamed Drouck.

"Oh my god, it's Nia." The Queen was in total disbelief. She inched forward towards the dimly lit room to get a better look, checking out her surroundings in case she had to duck.

"I don't know who they were. They seemed to know Shift, and he was the one who led them to that lady you took. She's a Queen?"

"Again, with the lies. After all I have done for you, you leave with Shift and betray me. How did Shift know I had the Queen?"

"How would I know? You killed my mother and kidnapped me and kept me here. What do I owe you, Drouck? Nothing!" sobbed Nia.

"Don't change the subject. How could you betray me? You had a good life here and now I can't trust you. Take her to the dungeon. You know you can never leave me. You belong to me, Nia."

"I belong to no one, especially you. You call a good life being your slave? That's rich. You're nothing but a kidnapper and murderer."

"Get her out of here. I probably should have done to you what we did to Shift. I'll just have to ponder that thought now, Nia?" he growled, getting in her face. A small red glow started to appear in his eyes, sending chills up Nia's spine. She just kept quiet.

Drouck stormed off in a rage. He knew he would never physically hurt her. Emotionally, it was a different story. "How could she leave me after all I did for her?" he thought to himself. "I'll just leave her in the dungeon overnight and let her think about betraying me again. Now that I have planted that seed in her head, she will think twice about trying to escape again."

The Queen jumped into the dark room next door and hid. She watched as the two guards dragged her daughter towards the dungeon. She followed them down the hallway; all the while, Nia pleaded not to take her to the dungeon.

"Please don't do this. Drouck is out of his mind."

"Quiet!" snapped one of the guards.

"Hey, did you hear something?" The other guard wheeled around.

"No, I didn't."

"Take her to the dungeon. I know I heard something. I'll be right back."

"Let's go!" he grabbed her arm, shoving her ahead.

"Who's back there?" cried the guard. The hallway was barely lit, and he was having a hard time navigating. The guard managed to walk right by the Queen. Fearful that Nia and the guard would hear her, she let them enter the hall before she went after the first guard.

"I know you're here," he stated loudly.

The Queen pulled out a porcelain ball she 'borrowed' from Keewae. As she snuck after the first guard, the ball transformed itself into a long stick resembling a baseball bat.

"Clever and perfect," she thought to herself.

"I know someone is there," cried the guard again.

"Someone is," replied the Queen, swinging away and knocking him down. She waited for a second to make sure he wasn't getting up. He wasn't. She smiled, twirled her newly formed weapon, and continued ahead.

The Queen caught up with Nia and the last guard.

"Just let me go, please," begged Nia.

The guard was walking behind Nia with his hand on her neck. "Walk!" he barked.

All of a sudden, the guard fell forward and landed on top of Nia.

"Ahhh, what are you doing?"

"Nia, Nia," whispered the Queen as she pulled the guard off her. "Are you alright?"

"It's you! My word... what are you doing here and that too, all by yourself? Where are the others? Are you really a Queen?" Nia was so startled she was rambling.

"Yes, I am alone, and yes, I am a Queen, but we must get out of here now. I will explain everything to you, but we are in serious danger as long as we are here. We need to get back to the trees before they disappear."

"Trees... disappear? What do you mean?"

"I'll explain later." The Queen helped Nia up, stroked her face, and grabbed her hand. "Hurry now." They ran towards the servant quarters to escape once again—this time, with her daughter by her side.

CHAPTER 24

Upon reaching upstairs, Sleet was looking well, which was a relief for Chuck. Corga and Sin Sin had already saddled Sleet and the rest of the Arabians for their journey ahead. "Again, my gratitude for saving Sleet, all of you," thanked Chuck.

"It was our honor Sir Charles, and I can speak for all of us," Corga replied.

"You kids, be careful. I don't have to tell you to keep the network of messages going. It is more important than ever right now," instructed Keewae.

"We are monitoring it at all times, Uncle," assured Corga.

So, for the second time, they packed up the horses and set out for the danger ahead of them. The Magic Forest was about half a mile from Keewae's den, so they got there in no time.

"This path, as you can see," said Keewae, "is made up of ancient lava."

"What are those markings on the lava? Is that Japanese hiragana!" Kehi was shocked.

"Why yes, Kehi. We have been trying to decipher each marking. We think these characters provide a clue to something, but what is the mystery we don't know? Since certain portions of the path are still covered throughout the forest, we are unable to piece together the whole puzzle."

"Has anyone tried uncovering them?"

"No, since The Magic Forest is too dangerous, no one will venture in to even try. Anyway, I cannot express enough not to wander off this path. Let me just say I have come close to dying a few times by taking this forest for granted and not staying on the path."

While Keewae was warning everybody of the dangers, Kehi took out a scroll and copied down the few markings that were exposed, hoping to find more as they went along. Chuck, noticing his friend, whispered, "Kehi, what do those mean?"

"I'll explain later," was all he stated.

"What do you mean?" Salair asked, not noticing Kehi.

"This forest contains exotic and rare botanicals. Plants you have never seen before. That is the lure of The Magic Forest. It will draw you off the path to admire its beauty or inhale the fragrances you are experiencing now. Stay on the path. It's beautiful but deadly. If you start feeling that urge, say something, as nothing in this forest is safe. That is why this forest is one of the few that hasn't been engulfed by the dark forces."

Keewae continued. "For the most part, the hornets rule this forest. Their pollination of all the vegetation contributes to the vast beauty that surrounds us. You will see them flying around. They are on patrol if you will. They may fly by and look friendly, but they are anything but that. They will harm anyone who tries to mess with or destroy their forest. If you get stung by these hornets, you will fall into an endless sleep, never to awaken. Individuals come in here and never come out. I have heard many screams at night coming out of here."

"My father and mother told me stories about The Magic Forest, but I thought they were fairy tales."

"No, Salair, this is not a fairy tale."

"I see that now," she said.

"We'll keep our guard up," said Chuck. "Keewae, lead the way."

The forest was filled with beautiful flowers of every color you could imagine, and long flowering vines hung off the trees. Keewae told everyone they would have to spend the night in a certain species of tree called the Snorfus. They are the friendliest trees in the forest, and at night, they actually snore.

"Why do we have to sleep in a tree?" asked the Princess.

Keewae replied, "At night, there are creatures that crawl on the ground that we do not want to ever come in contact with."

"Dare I ask what kind?" inquired Chuck.

"You know the red spiders back there you fought off? These are another off-shoot of Octimus's – black creatures with furry red, black legs and sharp teeth. They come looking for anyone or anything that was stung by the hornet or not lucky enough to make it out of the forest by nightfall. That is why the forest looks so clean. These creatures eat the unfortunates as you will."

"Like vultures."

"Correct, Chuck."

"Lovely!" the Princess shuttered.

Chuck noticed her shutter, "Not to worry Princess. You have four brave men to protect you."

"Well, three men and a fuzzar, I believe?" she replied. They all laughed.

The first day passed without anything unusual happening. It was starting to get a little dark, and Keewae said they ought to start looking for a Snorfus to spend the night in. They walked on and came across a very large Snorfus. In a low booming voice, it asked, "What are you doing in my forest?" Everyone stopped dead in their tracks.

"It is good to see you!" said Keewae.

"I thought you got swallowed up by the fungus pond," Mightus chuckled.

"Well, you know me Mightus, I put up a fight that nasty pond will never forget."

"I don't doubt that, my friend." The whole tree shook from laughter. "Why on earth would you be in The Magic Forest? Did you not learn your lesson last time?"

"We are on a very important journey and must get through the forest as quickly as possible. Care if we spend the night?"

"The more the merrier, my friend. You better get up here right now before it gets any darker. I don't need to tell you what happens. We can talk about your journey later tonight."

As everyone climbed up, the Princess noticed what looked like engravings of butterflies, but something even more unusual was that the engravings had a very light turquoise sparkle to them. These markings went all the way up the trunk of the tree. "Interesting," she thought to herself. "Again, with the turquoise." With the help of the old Snorfus, everybody, including the horses, got up safely and were comfortably settled. Mightus indeed fit his name as he was the largest and wisest tree in the forest. He had befriended Keewae years ago when Keewae ran into trouble with the night creatures.

"So," said Keewae, "might I make my introductions? These are my traveling companions. This is Princess Salair, her personal protector and Commander, Sasha Albion, Sir Charles and Kehi, Sir Charles' right-hand man, so to speak, and last but not least, is Berra. She belongs to Sir Charles."

"Exquisite bird, quite exquisite. My honor to have such distinguished guests with me. This is most unexpected, to say the least," said Mightus. "I don't believe I have ever been in the midst of bodyguard protection. Why the need?"

They filled Mightus in about finding Chuck, about Shift and their dumb luck in finding the Queen and the discovery of Nia, and then the Queen disappearing again to find Nia. They kept their word, and nothing was uttered about the discovery of the turquoise flower.

"We would ask, however, if you could keep a pulse on the whereabouts of the Queen, if possible?" inquired Keewae. My niece and nephews are doing the same through their resources, but you and the other Snorfus have always been helpful to us as well.

"Of course, anything for the Pishtar family. I do know from the rumblings in the forest that Drouck is gaining strength again and that he has several foes who are willing to back him. I hope your mother doesn't run into any trouble. I can't believe she would go out alone, very dangerous, very dangerous indeed," Mightus stated while shaking his trunk in disapproval.

"I feel the same way, Mightus. I am very worried about my mother, but she is headstrong. She snuck out on all of us."

"She must be very crafty to escape Keewae, let alone his mud home."

"More than I knew." Keewae chimed in.

Eager to change the subject, the Princess inquired, "Might I ask about the butterfly pattern up your trunk? What is that exactly?"

Mightus' whole trunk went a little limp.

"I am sorry, I should not have inquired."

"No, it's okay. The impressions were left by one of my very best friends. A dear friend I have not seen in quite a while." Mightus paused a minute and added, "Years ago, I befriended a beautiful butterfly. One day, Porcelain, that was her name, landed on my branch and was sobbing. We talked for a while. She thanked me and flew away. After that, she came back every day, always sad. She told me she had an older stepsister who was very, very cruel to her. We developed a great friendship."

"She sounds lovely," said the Princess.

"Porcelain was the most beautiful butterfly I have ever seen. She was turquoise, like a peacock. Regal. You would know her right away if you ever saw her. Anyway, she used to lie on her back when talking to me. When she flew away after our talks, her imprint was left on my trunk."

"Extraordinary! She is truly special. She is part of you."

"Yes. Thank you, Princess. I haven't told anyone about her."

"What happened to her Mightus?" asked Mr. Kehi.

"I don't know. She just stopped coming. I hope her sister didn't hurt her or worse. Sadly, it is the only thing I can think of."

"We will keep an eye out for her," Salair replied.

"Right, Chuck?" she looked at him with hope in her eyes.

"Yes, of course."

"I must admit I am very tired and wish to sleep for a little while.

"Of course," said Mightus. "You may climb right up there into that niche and the rest of you, as you wish." Surprisingly, Mightus had formed individual hammocks for everyone out of his silky leaves and cradling branches.

It wasn't long before Chuck woke up after hearing some rustling down below. He decided to climb to a better vantage point, only to discover Keewae and Sasha. They all glanced at each other and looked down. True to Keewae's description, Octimus's creatures were covering the area, eating up anything that got caught up in their wake. It was a frightening sight.

"Is there some sort of secret why they aren't climbing up here?" said Kehi.

"I will tell you," said Keewae, "the reason the Snorfus have survived the forest for so long is that the spiders have learned that climbing up any of these trees is deadly to them. You see, the Snorfus trees have a unique sensory system inherent in their species. These creatures especially set off their alarm system, if you will, triggering an excretion of poisonous sap. The spiders have adapted to the fact that they will not survive the climb and therefore respect the tree for its protective nature."

"Part of the allure of The Magic Forest," commented Sasha.

"It is, Sasha. So now you know that if you ever got caught at night in The Magic Forest, the Snorfus is your best friend."

"Pretty sure, that's not on my schedule anytime soon, Keewae."

"Mine either," Sasha laughed.

Early next morning, they had breakfast of muffins and some wonderful fruit they picked out of the forest (with Keewae's help, of course), which was green in color, shaped like a star, and tasted like cotton candy. Keewae dined on some purple beetles and swirly caterpillars he had captured.

"Mightus," said Keewae, "thank you for your hospitality. It was great to see you, old friend."

"Pleasure was all mine. I have contacted the Snorfus family and don't hesitate to stay with any of them."

"You are most kind," the Princess said as she stroked his nose.

"Oh, of course!" Mightus crinkled his nose shyly. "Anytime, Your Highness."

The forest was bright that day, although no one knew how the light got through the dense canopy. They decided to walk, leaving the horses as fresh as possible. Chuck was worried, however. They had not seen any of Prince Drouck's manras since they entered the forest, and he thought that was unusual because they have ways of getting through just about anything.

As they walked along, Kehi noticed the hiragana markings were becoming more prevalent. Again, Kehi took out his paper and copied the markings, mumbling to himself. He was stirred out of his thoughts momentarily.

"Princess," said Chuck. "I would feel better if you would ride one of the horses and stay off the ground."

"Just a bit further. I like the walk."

"Not too much further, Salair," warned Sasha. "This is no ordinary walk."

The forest was most beautiful, with unusually brilliant flowers, cactus trees with colorful blossoms, waterfalls, and creatures of all sorts everywhere. The forest smelled of pine and sweet flowers.

"The smells are incredible in this forest, Keewae," said the Princess.

"That is the danger of this place. It is beautiful in here but deadly."

"I agree, Salair. I thought my rose garden was fragrant, but this is unreal." Even Berra seemed to be taking in the smells as she sat on Chuck's shoulder and whistled some unusual notes no one had ever heard. The day wore on as they kept walking. Chuck was particularly nervous as he knew their beautiful surroundings were too good to be true.

"Ouch!" cried the Princess. "Ow!" she said. "What is that thing?" she asked, holding her ankle.

"Oh no," said Keewae as he stabbed the spiked creature that resembled a blowfish on legs, killing it.

"What was that?" cried Chuck.

"It is a red orbus, a very poisonous creature. I don't know what it's doing here on the path. They are usually found in the cool, damp areas of the forest. This creature had to have been planted here. This is very bad, very bad," stated Keewae as he started pacing.

The Princess stared briefly at Keewae, turned very pale, and collapsed into Chuck's arms.

"Keewae! What's going on? Has she been poisoned by that thing?" cried Sasha.

"I'm afraid so. This is bad. First, this poison paralyzes you, then it seeps into your bloodstream and slowly kills you."

"This can't be happening! How long does she have."

"I'm not sure, Chuck. One, maybe two days, max."

"Every poison has a remedy. There has got to be one, right, Keewae?" asked Kehi.

"Yes, Kehi. The only remedy I know to counteract the poison is to swallow the eggs of the fuzzy white caterpillar.

"Where exactly can we find these eggs?" asked Sasha.

"The only place you can get these eggs is from a castle ruled by Queen Morphina."

"And where can we find this Morphina character?" asked Sasha.

"She hides in a neighboring forest along with another character named Coridon. Together, they rule over all the beetle and caterpillar species in their forest. Morphina is bitter and cruel, part caterpillar, part butterfly. The two of them are keen allies of the octospy and Prince Drouck."

"Great. Why the fuzzy white caterpillar?" asked Kehi.

"The red orbus hatches from the cocoon spun by the fuzzy white caterpillar."

"Hence, the poison and the antidote," said Chuck.

"Correct," said Keewae.

"Well, I don't care who she is. We have no choice and no time to waste. We must do something immediately!" Chuck said, panicked.

"I agree, Chuck, but it's not like we can just go up to her and say, "Hey, can we have some eggs?" Even if we could, I have no actual idea where her castle is. And she will kill us, no questions asked."

"Excuse me," interrupted a tiny voice.

"I am afraid..." Keewae continued as Berra let out a sharp note.

"What is it, Berra?" Chuck asked.

"Excuse me," repeated a tiny voice.

"Did you hear something?" asked Kehi.

"No but, ah look, Kehi," replied Chuck as a stunningly beautiful butterfly landed on his shoulder.

Her body was tiny, but her large turquoise wings reminded one of a majestic peacock. Upon seeing the butterfly, Berra began to sing a song to the butterfly. Lifting her head as if listening to Berra's beautiful symphony, at the same time, the butterfly's wings took on a stunning turquoise glow. Just after Berra sang her last note, the butterfly landed on Berra's shoulder and fluttered her wings in understanding.

Everyone looked at each other, totally dumbfounded. All attention was focused on Berra and the butterfly.

"What is this?" Kehi whispered almost reverently.

"No idea," whispered Chuck, looking over at Kehi.

"Let me guess... Porcelain?" asked Keewae.

"Why yes, how would you know my name?" she inquired.

"We've met your good friend, Mightus," Keewae replied.

"You know Mightus?"

"He was kind enough to let us stay with him last night," Chuck chimed in. "Listen Porcelain, my name is Chuck, and these are my friends, Kehi, Keewae, and Sasha. This is Princess Salair, who, unbelievably, has been stung by a red orbus." He paused briefly, then, enlightened with intuition, said, "I think you know that, and I think that's why you came?"

"Yes, it is. She must get the antidote right away," Porcelain said alarmingly. "You understand, she will die."

"Yes, Porcelain," replied Keewae. "I am aware it's a deadly poison, but how can you help us? We need to get to Queen Morphina's castle for the antidote. I don't know if you know that or not, but... "

"I know exactly where her castle is," she stated, interrupting Keewae.

"How would you know about her castle?" asked Chuck.

"I would know because Queen Morphina is my stepsister, and she held me captive there until I escaped," she said matter-of-factly. "I can explain on the way. We must hurry. I can only tell you we will be in harm's way from here on out, so you must follow my instructions no matter how strange they may seem to you. The way to her castle is unfriendly and treacherous. But if we do not get those eggs, the Princess will surely perish. Queen Morphina must have sent that nasty orbus out. They are not in this part of the forest, as you know, Keewae."

"I thought as much," said Keewae.

"Lead the way, Porcelain. I don't care how dangerous it is," insisted Chuck.

"Dodge!" Porcelain yelled out. "Dodge, come here."

"Who's Dodge?" inquired Keewae.

"He is my friend and protector. He befriended me after I escaped from the castle. He can be a little cranky at times, but he means well." Dodge came dive-bombing in on Keewae as he was a little too close to Porcelain.

"Whoa, little fella," exclaimed Keewae as he ducked. "We're on your side." Keewae turned his head to study the yellow bird who hovered above Porcelain, keeping his little furrowed brow on Keewae. Dodge was a bright yellow hummingbird with a black head and the most belligerent attitude to match.

"Dodge, stop it. Behave yourself. These people are friendly," said Porcelain. "He is a descendant of the rarest breeds of hummingbirds. His ancestors fought in battles alongside the giant eagles. That's where he got the attitude you're seeing, Keewae."

"Impressive little guy, I must say, Porcelain."

Porcelain proceeded with more information. "There's a Snorfus about a mile away. He is expecting us."

"Let's go, Dodge. Keep a lookout, if you would." Dodge flew off in a blaze. Berra launched off Chuck's shoulder and caught up with Dodge.

"Wow," said Keewae. "I don't think I have ever seen anything like that."

"Yes," said Porcelain, "there is no one like Dodge. He is fierce despite his size. I am lucky to have him. Speaking of birds, where did you find your bird? She is quite rare."

"I stumbled upon her a long time ago. She must be very rare as I have never seen another one like her."

"Trust me, she is, and no, you haven't. Let's get to the Snorfus ASAP."

Chuck was perplexed by that comment and wanted to ask her about the interchange between them, but the Princess was a priority right now.

"Let's go, Keewae." Chuck jumped on Sleet's back and said, "Here, lift the Princess up to me." Kehi lifted up the Princess to Chuck. "Lead the way, Porcelain." They all mounted the horses and sped off at a fast clip toward the next Snorfus.

Chuck was beside himself as the Princess wasn't moving at all. "If she dies, I will never forgive myself. I should have made her get on a horse," he thought to himself.

Before long, Porcelain descended to fly alongside Chuck and announced, "We're here!" They stopped before another huge sprawling tree. "The horses must stay here also."

With the life of the Princess at stake, Chuck was not going to argue. The only thing he could do was trust Porcelain and do exactly as she stipulated.

The tree flapped its huge, leafy branches and rumbled, "I am Anglus. Mightus has notified us all to expect you and assist where we can. I am honored to help the Princess and her friends. This is a great travesty, Queen Morphina sabotaging the Princess this way. Everyone will be safe with me."

"Thank you, Anglus," said Keewae.

Chuck rested the unconscious Princess on the giant swaying leaf and stared at her briefly, resting a hand on her cheek. "We'll be back, Sasha. You have my word; we will save her."

Anglus lifted Sasha, Salair, and the horses up with great ease. "You must hurry," he urged them.

"Let's go, Porcelain," Chuck said. Chuck, Kehi and Keewae took off with Porcelain to the Queen's castle. As they were running, Keewae observed Chuck closely. He felt sure he knew why Chuck had that determined yet wild look in his eye, with his jaw set in a hard line.

"Chuck, don't blame yourself. We were all there with the Princess. Besides, the red orbus is never on a path. It thrives in darkness and dampness. It was the work of evil."

Overhearing those words, Porcelain added, "Yes, it was my stepsister. Keewae is right. There is no mistaking of her evilness." Porcelain went on. "She has hourglass beetles everywhere. They must have informed her that you were in the forest, and she sent the red orbus out."

"How would she even know?" asked Kehi.

"My sister is friends with the oldest hourglass beetle in her kingdom. She is kept in a secret location that only Morphina knows about. This particular beetle, whose name is Coridon, is a creepy, slimy beetle who preyed upon Queen Morphina as a youngster and whose only goal was to take over the castle and be the rightful heir to King Willow's kingdom. Morphina can look on Coridon's back and the entire network of her beetles is displayed there. They are strewn all over the forest. She can pick a beetle, and it displays that part of the forest. That's how they can tell who is coming and going. If they don't like what is coming, they are snuffed out. Not many intruders come into this part of the forest anyway. It's pretty well hidden."

"Maybe we should come back and find Coridon some other time," Keewae muttered under his breath.

"Morphina would certainly be at a great disadvantage, to say the least, if something were to happen to Coridon," said Porcelain.

"Since my colors are so bright," said Porcelain, "to my disadvantage sometimes, I must fly fairly high in order to stay above the eyesight of the Queen's beetles. I will keep ahead of you. Please do not look up to look for me, as I will be detected. When I stop in a certain area above, that would mean I have spotted an hourglass beetle. Berra and Dodge will fly with me and chirp when you are upon one. You must kill it before it sees you. At least this way, we can make a path to come back where we know we won't be spied on."

"Okay, Porcelain," replied Chuck. "This sounds pretty dicey to me, but it is our only option, correct?"

"Yes, unfortunately. This part of the path has the least number of beetles, but I am afraid it is the most dangerous. Let's go, Dodge." Dodge came whizzing by everyone and stayed right on Porcelain's tail along with Berra.

"We understand," said Keewae. "Lead the way." Off went Porcelain, Dodge, and Berra.

"What a unique threesome," said Kehi.

"Impressive," nodded Chuck.

They all followed Porcelain, all the while admiring her regal beauty.

Chuck thought it was a shame she had such an evil stepsister—quite the opposite of the beautiful creature in front of them.

Keewae's tentacles on top of his head were sensing alarm. "Slow down guys; there must be one up here." Sure enough, just ahead, Porcelain was hovering. Before they could attack it, Berra dove straight down into it, striking it dead.

"Look," said Kehi as Berra flew up ahead of them and then dove straight down again, taking out another beetle.

With the help of Keewae's alarm system, Berra and company found it much easier to locate the hourglass beetles and destroy them as they went along.

Porcelain doubled back and was hovering above the threesome. "Impressive," she whispered, "although not surprising." Porcelain was off again with Dodge on her tail. "There she goes again with those intriguing comments." Chuck thought to himself. Chuck held up his arm as Berra was happy to have a landing. As she rested on his arm, he stared at her with a smile. She bowed her head and jumped back onto his shoulder.

"We are being watched," whispered Kehi.

"Kehi, if you see something shiny or reflective in this dark, damp place, it is probably them."

They continued in silence, walking and stabbing.

Of course, only Keewae was walking, stabbing, and eating, all the while commenting on how tasty they were.

They finally stopped at what looked like the wall that surrounded the castle, a very high wall. "This is the back area. She doesn't have this area guarded very well."

CHAPTER 25

"What happened to my beetles?" screeched Queen Morphina.

"Someone or something has taken out our eyes on the west side of the forest," hissed Coridon. "This could only mean your pathetic stepsister is back for something. She has company with her, including a fuzzar, a very dangerous creature. The beetles went dark before I could make out who else was with her. And if I can't see my area, it means my beetles are dead. You better take care of this, Samantha. No one breaches my kingdom without being punished. No one leaves this castle alive. Do you hear me? Find out what happened. Get out!"

As Morphina started to say something, she was cut off. "Get out I said… Now!" yelled Coridon.

Morphina knew when to be quiet and ran out of Coridon's quarters, taking her servant Yashi with her.

"Yashi, get Gouda for me immediately. The only person who knows about my hourglass beetle system is my ungrateful stepsister. My red orbus must have done the trick and poisoned someone they know. She would never come back to face me unless it were a dire situation, and they needed the antidote."

"It would take some doing to take out that many beetles," commented Yashi.

"Well, Coridon said she was with a fuzzar. They are ferocious creatures, so that would explain a lot. Go get Gouda like I asked you," snapped Morphina.

"Yes, ma'am!"

Morphina's leader of the horned-rimmed beetles, Gouda, came strolling in. "I hear we may have visitors. You asked to see me, my Queen?"

"Yes, Gouda. We are under attack on the west side. Apparently, Porcelain has brought a fuzzar with her, and she is headed this way. Take the horned-rimmed beetles with you and get rid of it and whoever else he may be with. Do not harm Porcelain. She will be punished for this, and that would be my responsibility," she said, grinningly.

"Of course, my Queen, right away," he said and ran off to follow orders. "I'll take extra beetles," he thought, as he didn't like the fact that a fuzzar was inside the kingdom.

"After all this time Yashi, I finally get to punish Porcelain for escaping the castle."

Yashi kept her feelings to herself. She liked Porcelain and it was hard to watch how cruel Morphina was to her. Yashi was hoping to escape from her for good one day. The less she said, the better it was for her.

"Why would she be with a fuzzar of all things? I have never seen one before. This is most curious," Morphina stated while her body colors fluctuated. "Just in case, we better up the guard number tonight. A fuzzar..." pondered the Queen.

"Yes, ma'am. I will see to it."

CHAPTER 26

"What now, Porcelain? We can't climb this wall, obviously," asked Chuck.

"You three stand side by side if you would and lean against the wall," she said.

They just looked at each other and complied. Porcelain flew up and over the wall and pressed herself into a stone with a matching butterfly indentation. The wall took on a dull turquoise glow, engulfing Chuck, Kehi, and Keewae. Berra's turquoise feathers took on a similar dull glow.

"Step backward now!" Porcelain cried. They obliged, and taking a step back, they went through the wall like it wasn't even there. The glow disappeared, and they found themselves inside the castle grounds.

"That's impossible Porcelain. How did you do that?" cried Kehi.

"I'll explain later. We must hurry." She just wanted to get what they came for and get out. She was scared and worried but knew she must help the Princess.

"I don't know if there is an explanation for that," mumbled Chuck.

"One more obstacle. There's a gate just ahead," Porcelain warned from above.

"Hold up," murmured Keewae as he held his paw up. His long claw came out, and before anyone knew it, another beetle was sliced in half. Keewae gulped the beetle down in two bites, smacking his lips delightfully.

Kehi's jaw dropped, and he said, "Happy now?"

"You have no idea," Keewae said.

"Thank you, Keewae," whispered Porcelain. "This way," she whispered to them. They came up to an old gate of entangled branches.

"This is the gate leading to the main castle," said Porcelain and asked them to wait for a moment while she fluttered wildly in front of the latch.

"What is she doing?" whispered Chuck. Just then, the latch made a clicking sound.

"Now!" she said, "Push the gate open." Kehi pushed on the gate, and it swung open.

"Hurry," said Porcelain as they ran through. The gate shut with a vengeance as if trying to take them out.

"Whoa," said Kehi.

"I am sorry, but this gate only knows me and is quite aware of intruders. Follow me," Porcelain apologized.

Concerned about the time, Chuck was becoming restless. It seemed that everything was taking so much of the precious hours allotted to them. "She is strong!" with this positive thought, he dismissed all the negative ones and prayed she would still be alive upon their return.

CHAPTER 27

Gouda, Queen Morphina's head beetle, came into the Queen's quarters. "My Queen, the beetles on our west side have been wiped out."

"Porcelain and the fuzzar?" questioned Morphina in a harsh tone.

"Well, whoever it was, they are gone. We didn't see anyone around," responded Gouda.

"Take more horned beetles back out and hunt down who did this Gouda. This has never happened before. I'll check with Coridon and see if she sees anything. I trust you'll know what to do with these trespassers when you find them. Now hurry."

"Of course, we will take care of them... swiftly," grinned Gouda. "I will keep you informed."

"Coridon has also lost track of them, my Queen," Yashi reported.

"I'll go talk to her. Summon the bees, Yashi. Tell Yellowjacket I want to see him immediately."

"Yellowjacket, ma'am?"

"Do you have a problem, Yashi? Are you questioning me?"

"No, my Queen, of course not."

"Do as I say. Now go!"

CHAPTER 28

"Okay, you guys, one more wall to get through. This will make it easier to avoid further detection. Stand over there, please," instructed Porcelain. Keewae, Kehi, and Chuck looked questionably at one another but followed her instructions.

"Here we go." Porcelain fluttered her wings in fervor in front of the wall. Berra noticed that Porcelain was struggling. Berra worried and wondered if Porcelain was the true conduit of the turquoise chain, so she flew over to Porcelain and stared at her. It was a message. Porcelain knew she had to keep going no matter what happened with her stepsister. She looked at Berra, gave her a nod, and began fluttering her wings with purpose now. With Berra looking on with feathers aglow, it gave Porcelain the courage she needed to carry on. Feeling her power, she summoned the light within her, which made her wings glow so brightly that everyone had to shield their eyes. Having witnessed this before, Dodge shot straight up in the air to avoid the bright flash. Everything went dark after the bright flash. Magically, they had landed in a small, musty room inside the castle.

"We are now in the castle," said Porcelain.

"Big magic, Porcelain," exclaimed Keewae.

"I have a few powers of my own that she does not know about. Nor does she know about the wall or this room. We must be very careful from here on out, as her guards are everywhere."

Chuck looked over at Kehi. "Ancient powers, if I'm not mistaken," he said under his breath, "once again, the interaction between Berra and Porcelain. Did you see Berra's feathers?"

Kehi nodded in agreement, "Ancient powers, yes. Very curious. Two separate magical powers working together. Can't explain any of it."

Chuck cracked the door open. "All clear," he whispered.

"Follow me," said Porcelain. "Dodge, stay behind me."

She led them into a pitch-black hallway. The only source of light was the glow of her wings, which they silently followed. Suddenly, Porcelain's wings darkened, and a rancid, mild smell permeated the air.

"Beetle guards ahead," whispered Porcelain.

Chuck and Kehi drew their swords. The smell grew more pungent, and they knew the sentries were close.

"Now," trilled Porcelain, sending a flicker of light to her wings. Chuck could see just enough to swing his sword, lopping off the head of one beetle. Though Kehi was preparing to administer a treatment similar to the other, Keewae reached him first, stabbing him with his razor-sharp talon and dropping the beetle to his fate.

"Well done," enthused Porcelain. "Morphina must know we are here. Hurry. This way."

They crept along the dark halls and occasionally ran into a few more beetles who met the same fate as the first ones.

"Here we are, just around this corner," said Porcelain.

As Porcelain started to round the corner, she stopped abruptly and fluttered backwards. "There are two guards at the entrance of the egg room. These are my sister's Scandinavian horned beetles. They resemble upright triceratops. They have an incredibly hard shell. They are almost impossible to kill. Not to forget, they are brutal and very mean. They may be mean, but unfortunately for Queen Morphina, they are not very smart."

"Porcelain," said Chuck, "can you fly above those beetles and distract them away from the door without being caught?"

"Yes, I can," she said.

"Good, while you do that, we will break into the egg room."

"Be careful, Porcelain," warned Keewae. "Let's go." Porcelain's wing lit up, and she slowly started flying towards the guards. Porcelain fluttered about their faces and got them pretty worked up. She took off, keeping just out of their reach. As they followed her down the hall, Chuck, Keewae, and Kehi approached the door. Using his long, powerful claw, Keewae broke the lock off the door.

"You guys guard the door while I grab the eggs."

Chuck entered the room and was floored by the hundreds and hundreds of jarred eggs. "What the heck could she be saving all these eggs for?" he muttered under his breath. He grabbed a couple of containers and headed for the door.

"Okay, I got some," said Chuck. "Any sign of Porcelain?"

"No, but I think our friends are coming back. Let's go. I am sure Porcelain will meet us at the wall if she doesn't see us," said Kehi.

"Come on then," replied Chuck.

"Was that the Queen's sister we were just chasing?" asked one beetle to the other.

"I am not sure; she hasn't been seen around here in years. Why would she come back here anyway, unless... I have a bad feeling. Hurry." They ran to the egg room only to discover the broken lock.

"Oh no. The Queen will punish us for this when she finds out we have intruders. Check inside."

The guard went in and came out immediately. "They stole some eggs! Sound the alarm."

Chuck, Kehi, and Keewae reached the room where they entered with Porcelain. But there was no sign of Porcelain.

"I have a bad feeling," said Chuck. "She should have been here by now."

"I agree," said Keewae, "but we have no time to spare. The Princess is dying, and we have the antidote. Chuck, take the eggs and go."

"Kehi and I will go back for Porcelain. But first, we have to find a way out of the castle since we can't get out of that room without Porcelain."

"Chuck," said Kehi, "I saw some stairs just out our door and to the left. Let's try those and see if they lead outside." What they found was a staircase leading downward.

"Man, it's dark," said Chuck, feeling his way ahead. "Stay against the wall guys." They started descending the staircase. The wall at their back was covered in vines that got thicker as they descended. The leaves began rustling the further down they went.

"It's beginning to get too thick to get through guys. What is going on with these vines?" asked Chuck.

"What a minute, Chuck. Trade places with me." Once Keewae got in front, he ran his paws through the vines and his antennas were not alarming him, quite the opposite.

"What is it, Keewae?" asked Kehi.

"This is interesting. These are the same vines that encompass my area." Keewae leaned back onto the thicket of vines and disappeared.

"What the heck? Where did he go? Keewae?" cried Chuck.

"Right here, Chuck." He reappeared.

"Was that a trick? How did you do that?" asked Kehi.

"No trick, Kehi. These are roughly the same vines that surround my house. Very friendly, very friendly indeed."

"Maybe to you," said Chuck. "How would the same vines be friendly to us? We are the trespassers. The vines at your house protect against intruders, obviously. Remember what they did to us when we entered your property? Wouldn't they have the same reaction to protect the Queen at her castle?"

"I think if the Queen knew about these vines, they would react quite differently. I'm wondering how this species got here in the first place."

"Maybe it is guarding someone else besides the Queen, who is friendly?" stated Kehi.

Keewae stared at Kehi for a second, "Brilliant thought, Kehi. I would never have thought about that."

"Brilliant is right, but who?" asked Chuck. "We'd better get going and figure that out later. All right, Keewae. You know we trust you. Let's go."

They looked over at Keewae as he leaned back and once again disappeared through the vines.

Chuck looked at Kehi, "Ready for this, Kehi?"

"Why not... Friendly vines. Count me in."

"Wow!" Chuck exclaimed. "Good thing you were with us Keewae; we couldn't have done that without you."

"Right. We would have no way of knowing those vines were friendly. And look," said Kehi, "we're back at the wall. Since Porcelain isn't around, your climbing prowess will have to kick in. You must go now as fast as you can."

"I hate leaving you guys to find Porcelain, but I have no choice," said Chuck. "If you don't come back in the morning, I am coming back for you."

"I'm hoping we'll find her right away. I hope nothing has happened to her," said Keewae.

"Yeah, we probably shouldn't have sent her as a distraction by herself. That was stupid." Kehi was angry.

"Just find her, Kehi. Give me a hand up, would you?"

They hoisted Chuck halfway up the wall. It was high and hard to get a foothold. Keewae and Kehi waited. It took a few minutes, but he managed to scale the rest of the way up and disappeared from Kehi and Keewae's sight.

"Good luck, my friend," whispered Kehi.

"Berra," said Chuck, "lead the way and keep an eye out for the hourglass beetles." Berra nodded and flew higher to get a better view. They had cleared a good path on the way to the castle, so it was pretty quiet going back. Occasionally, Berra made a couple of dives, taking out a few hourglass beetles as they went. Berra was flying at a heated pace with Chuck right beside her, admiring her sheer beauty and strength.

"God, I hope I get to the Princess in time," he thought to himself. It was starting to get dark, which added to his alarm.

The poison was slowly taking over the Princess. She was very pale, and the veins in her leg where the orbus stung her had started turning black. She lay in Sasha's arms and stared at him, blinking occasionally.

Sasha just held her, watching her, and silently pleading, "Please Chuck, please get here."

"Sasha, I'm not sure they are going to make it back in time," she whispered in a faint voice.

"If I know anything, Chuck will be here. Just hang in there, Princess." Sasha was in anguish as he watched the Princess' eyes close once more. She was silent and motionless. He waited and waited. The black venom in her veins was slowly making its way towards her heart.

Finally, a flicker of long eyelashes and a weak, halting voice, "Sasha, tell my parents that I love them and will always be with them no matter… "

"No, Princess! Please stay with me."

She lay perfectly still. Her eyes gradually reopened. "Sasha, you have always been a great friend to me and, for that, I am forever grateful." The Princess closed her eyes again.

"No, Princess, please. I know Chuck is coming." He waited, fearful, hoping, holding his breath, staring at a perfectly still face and noticing the black venom now at the base of her neck.

"This is not happening. Stay with me, Princess, please," he pleaded.

"Tell Chuck..." she tried to speak but lapsed into silence. Sasha leaned over her, trying to hear the words. He heard nothing.

Anglus saw Berra and Chuck coming, "Hurry, Chuck, she's fading!"

Stretching out his longest limb, Anglus scooped him up and planted him right next to the Princess and Sasha.

"Oh, thank God, Chuck! Hurry! We're losing her!" Her breath was very faint.

Chuck was panting hoarsely. Soaked with perspiration, he ripped off his jacket, pulled the vials of eggs out of his pockets, and set them carefully by Sasha.

"Let me have her. Sasha open one of the vials; I'll hold her mouth."

"How much?"

"I don't know. Try half of the vial first." Sasha poured the eggs into her mouth.

"Just wait," he said, "she'll be okay."

As she lay there lifeless, Sasha said after about a minute, "Nothing is happening, Chuck."

"Let me try the rest of the vial," Sasha said, pouring the rest into her mouth. Again, they waited, nothing. Salair remained motionless.

"She's gone. We're too late." Tears were welling up in Sasha's dark eyes.

Chuck just stared at the beautiful girl in his arms.

Berra dropped down to a lower branch just above the head of the Princess and began to sing a low, eerily beautiful song – one Chuck had never heard before – its melody floating hauntingly through the forest. After singing, the Golden Bird flapped her wings wildly several times. Chuck and Sasha repeatedly jerked their inquisitive gazes from the ailing Princess back to Berra. Then they waited – Sasha fearing the Princess would ascend to the Nether World; Sir Charles adamant she would remain in this one.

A dead silence reigned. Both Sir Charles and Sasha were holding their breath. Neither dared move nor speak. Waiting. Watching.

"I should have watched her more closely," moaned Sasha, breaking the silence.

"I should have insisted she ride the horse," Chuck mumbled.

"Chuck, look!" as Sasha glanced over at the Princess.

Her eyes were moving ever so slightly under her eyelids.

This time, Berra flew off the branch and landed directly next to Salair. Again, she sang the same haunting melody, ending with the frantic wing flapping. The black venom started receding.

"Chuck, look! The venom is receding."

"Whatever she is doing, it's working? Come on Salair, come back to us."

Chuck just held Salair as he and Sasha stared at each other in amazement.

"What do you think that means, Chuck?"

"I couldn't even begin to tell you."

Salair stopped the eye movement. Berra just stared at her and waited.

Chuck and Sasha continued to beat themselves up on how they failed the Princess, not noticing that the Princess slowly opened her beautiful turquoise eyes and gazed into those of the Golden Bird. Berra's head nodded repeatedly at the Princess as their eyes remained locked with the familiar, faint turquoise glow emanating between them. The interaction of the rare egg and Berra's stare caused the poison to seep gradually but surely away from her body. She nodded at Berra with a slight but understanding smile. Satisfied the Princess was revived, Berra retreated to her perch.

Salair coughed weakly, leaving a tiny, turquoise droplet on her bottom lip.

"It was no one's fault," declared Salair as she looked up from Chuck's arms.

Chuck dropped his head to his chest, uttered a silent prayer of gratitude, and then hugged the Princess in relief.

"Princess!" exclaimed Sasha, anxious for reassurance as he hovered over them, "You're alright!" He glanced at Chuck with gratitude and disbelief.

"Yes, Sasha," she reached a hand to him, "I am fine… thanks to… was that Berra singing and whatever else happened?"

Chuck and Sasha simultaneously embraced her. She smiled faintly at them, then said to Chuck, "I know you… risked… your life to… save me… Thank you!"

"It was Berra. I have never heard anything like that," said Chuck.

"Maybe it was a song designed to work with the white caterpillar eggs to counteract the poison?" Sasha implied.

"Do you know how crazy that sounds, Sasha?"

"Crazy but not out of the realm of possibilities. She sings melodies, and magical things keep happening."

"I kept hearing one of the most unusual melodies, nothing like I've ever heard before. It was very strange, like it was beckoning me to come to the light."

"I have no doubt that is exactly what she was doing," replied Chuck.

Now that the Princess was becoming stronger, she lifted her head a bit to look around her. She saw the leaves, trunk, and branches of the Snorfus tree, and only Sasha and Chuck. "Where are the others?" she inquired.

"Porcelain disappeared while we were getting the eggs," explained Chuck.

"You found Porcelain?" whispered Salair.

"Oh yes. She found us and led us to her stepsister's castle, the only place with the remedy for the red orbus poison. But now we fear she has been captured. Kehi and Keewae went to look for her while I returned here. Their status is unknown as well."

"Oh no," tears welled up in her eyes, overcome with guilt. "My carelessness has put everyone in danger or worse."

"No, it was my fault, Princess," soothed a somber Sasha. "I was careless in looking out for you. I should be removed as your guardian."

"Don't be ridiculous, Sasha," said Chuck, "it was my fault. I never should have allowed her to get off Willow and walk in this dangerous place."

The Princess could barely keep her eyes open, "I think I need to rest now."

"Are you sure you're alright?"

"Yes, Chuck, I'm fine, thanks to you."

"I need to get back to the castle as quickly as possible. Sasha, guard her with your life."

"The Princess will be safe with me," rumbled Anglus, forcing the tumbling Berra to snag onto a lower branch. "Now that she is better, I will allow no harm to come to her."

"Oh, of course. Pardon me Anglus. I meant no disrespect, but it is getting late, and I must be on my way."

"Not tonight, Sir Charles. It is too close to getting dark, and you are well aware of what happens. I know you want to rescue your friends, but it would be better if you leave at first light."

"I forgot, Anglus. First light it is."

"You need some rest anyway, Chuck," said a worried Sasha. "You'll be much more effective in the morning."

"That is true."

Chuck and Sasha went out of earshot of the Princess.

"This is most distressing, Sasha. If it weren't for this god-forsaken forest at night, I would have gone back to the castle immediately."

"I know, but you should get a little rest. I think you are running on adrenaline right now. I just wish I could go with you."

"I know, Sasha, but obviously, you cannot. I will be able to get there faster this time as I'll be on horseback. Berra will be on the lookout for more hourglass beetles.

"Forgive me for eavesdropping," said Anglus.

"We have all been talking to Mightus about your travels. Our relatives are spread throughout the forest and will assist you as much as we can. Sapius is about twenty miles down the path and will be expecting you and the Princess. You will recognize him by the brightly colored sap around his trunk."

"The Princess and I can make it that far. We'll have the horses and their protection."

"Just stay on the lava path. I need not remind you what can happen," scolded Anglus.

"Trust me, Anglus, we've learned our lesson," snapped Sasha. He didn't like being scolded like a child.

"My apologies, sir," Anglus realized he was out of line.

"I know you're just trying to help, and we appreciate it, of course."

"Thank you, Anglus. I think we will all be on guard from now on," said Chuck.

Everyone rose early the next morning, eager to rescue their friends.

"Hopefully, this won't take too long to get into the castle and get everyone out safely. I'll plan to meet you at Sapius as soon as I can. If something happens, we can get a word through the Snorfus and keep in touch that way," Chuck instructed.

"Please be careful, Chuck," Salair said and hugged Chuck.

"I'll do my best," he said, gazing at the beautiful Princess, thankful for her recovery.

"We'll wait for you unless we get word otherwise," said Sasha. "I'm not happy you have to go alone, but you have Berra and three Arabian warrior horses, so that makes me feel a little better."

"Odds are in my favor, Sasha." Chuck smiled as he wheeled around. "See you soon." He galloped off with Berra soaring above.

Chuck rode Tarr and took Mirka and Shia with him. He was hoping the darker-colored horses would blend in with the dark of the forest. At least, this time, with the gift of night vision, the horses had no trouble making their way through the forest and back to the castle. He was going to have to figure out another way into the castle. Without Porcelain, magically, there was no way to get in.

CHAPTER 29

After Porcelain led the guards away from the egg room, she was heading back when she felt something thrown over her, taking her to the ground. As such, her femur suffered a break.

"Oh no," she cried in pain.

"Oh yes," said Gouda, Queen Morphina's head beetle. "Hello, my dear Porcelain. My, my! What brings you here? It's been a while. Oh, I'm sorry, did I hurt you?"

Porcelain noticed he was grinning at her expense. "Let me up, Gouda. This has nothing to do with you."

"Oh, but it does. Your stepsister will be so happy with me, catching her little intruder." Porcelain winced as the netting he threw over her was heavy.

Porcelain remained quiet. She feared Gouda and didn't want to antagonize him. She had been tortured by him before. You would never know what he was going to do to you.

"You're awfully quiet for a trespasser. Let's get you settled and see what happens."

He scooped the netting up with her in it and headed back to the dungeon area. Gouda did not carry her delicately, swinging her to and fro without regard to the rough ride. Dodge watched on, completely horrified, but knew he had to stay out of sight and keep an eye on where he was taking Porcelain. He followed silently behind Gouda. The rough ride to the dungeon didn't do Porcelain any favors. By the time they got there, besides her broken femur, one of her forewings was crushed.

Gouda dumped Porcelain out of the netting and onto a table. He then put a glass container over her and watched her squirm in pain.

"I see you haven't changed." Porcelain stated, trying to be brave.

"I'll be happy to report your capture to your lovely sister now," Gouda said, smirking as he left.

Seeing him leave, Dodge flew frantically around Porcelain's container, trying to figure out how to get the container off her. He pressed himself against the glass to try and push it over.

"It's okay, Dodge. You can't do this alone. Go find the others and stay out of sight. Morphina must not know about you or you being here."

Dodge looked at her, dejected. He knew she was right and reluctantly flew off at a heated pace to get help.

While all this was happening, the vines had pulled Kehi and Keewae back up to the castle. "These vines have been a great help to us," said Kehi. "We need to figure out where they go."

"Yes," said Keewae, "First things first, let's find Porcelain."

They climbed back up the stairs, reaching the doorway. Keewae cracked the door and peered out. Fortunately for them, the castle was lit with torches.

"Looks clear. Let's go, Kehi. Let's start at that end and work our way forward." They started searching each room, being careful to dodge any guards they encountered. Keewae was angry that he led them into harm's way, between the Princess, which he was unsure whether Chuck made it back to save her in time or not, and now, losing Porcelain, he was not in any mood to run into any beetles.

"Keewae, look. What is that coming at us? Can you make it out? It's not very big."

Kehi drew his sword.

"Wait. It's Dodge!" said Keewae.

"Dodge! Where's Porcelain?" whispered Kehi.

Dodge flew back and forth in front of them in a fervor.

"Lead the way, little buddy," urged Kehi.

He zoomed off in a hurry with his help following. They could barely keep up with him; he was flying so fast. Dodge knew there was no time to waste as Porcelain was in bad shape.

"There he is," whispered Kehi as Dodge zoomed into a dimly lit room just ahead of them.

"Up there," said Kehi. "Keewae, don't you think it is strange there are no guards around Porcelain?"

"It is. Something's not right." Keewae's tentacles were going bonkers, setting off alarm bells in his head. Keewae's long claw came out as he and Kehi crept closer. He peered in the door and saw Porcelain being held in a glass container. "Oh no, Porcelain."

"What is it?" whispered Kehi.

"It's Porcelain – she's been captured, and she's injured."

Kehi's blood was boiling now.

"I don't see anyone in there, but my alarm tentacles are going crazy."

"Maybe they are on their way? Let's grab her and get out of here."

They stepped into the room, not realizing the beetles had burrowed themselves into the wall, rendering them undetectable.

"Porcelain," whispered Keewae. She looked up.

"Oh no, Keewae, what are you doing here? You must get out of here right away. It's a trap!"

It was too late. The door slammed shut, and the guards engulfed her two friends.

CHAPTER 30

Chuck rode Mirka as fast as he could towards the magic wall. Shia and Tarr followed behind him. On his way, all he could think about was how to get everyone over the wall. He was hoping that Keewae, Kehi, and Porcelain were out by now. However, Chuck did not have a good feeling about it. He brushed his negative thoughts aside and was glad he was riding this time as opposed to walking. It made going back a lot faster this time. Between the horses and Berra, he was in good hands. They reached the wall without incident.

"Well, Mirka," whispered Chuck, "even with your jumping skills, the wall is way too high."

"Let's go down this direction towards the castle," Chuck suggested to Mirka. As the horses, Chuck and Berra crept along, it got darker and darker the closer they got to the castle.

"Berra, see if you can find an opening. Everyone is depending on us."

Just in front of them was another hourglass beetle that caught sight of them for just a moment until Mirka cut right through the beetle with his razor-sharp hooves.

"Good boy," said Chuck, "however, I am afraid we have now been seen. Hopefully, Berra will find something for us." Chuck had barely spoken those words when he saw Berra flying back and giving him a look and a low whistle.

"I knew you would find something. Let's go everyone." Berra led them along a high thistle hedge. As they ran forward, the hedges got a little lower until they came to a stone landing. Berra stopped at the landing and then flew straight across the moat to another opening directly across from where Chuck and the horses were standing. It was an opening to the castle.

"Nice work, Berra," whispered Chuck. He then cleared as long of a runway as he could for the stallions to run down.

"So guys, this is our only way in. We have to jump across." With their lightning speed, Chuck was confident they would make it across. The drop-off was death, and he knew it. Berra flapped her wings and whistled an alarmingly low note.

"What is it, Berra?"

Voices were now coming from the darkness.

"There they are. Spare no one! They'll never make it over the moat." A faint light was in the distance, and it was coming towards them at a rapid pace.

"There's no time like the present guys. Shia, you and Tarr go first. The gallant Arabians thundered down the pathway at a Herculean pace, then hurtled themselves high and far into the air. They cleared the moat with ease and now waited for Chuck and Mirka to get across. Chuck let out a big sigh of relief.

"Okay Mirka, it's our turn. Run like you've never run before." Chuck's heart was pounding as if beating out of his chest.

Chuck dug his heels into Mirka's side. Mirka took off at a furious pace, knowing he had the extra weight to carry across the moat. It was almost like time had stopped as they leaped from the edge of the moat. Mirka gave it a mighty leap. Leaning forward over Mirka's mane, Chuck tried to help him clear the moat.

Mirka reached the landing, albeit with his front hooves. His back legs, however, didn't quite get there. Even with his razor-sharp hooves, they hardly managed to dig into the cliff's edge and started slipping backwards. Mirka kept pedaling his back legs, but Chuck knew they weren't going to make it. Witnessing the whole thing, Berra snatched a rope with her beak off Tarr's saddle and wrapped the rope around the saddle horns of both Tarr and Shia. She let out a cry and flew directly at Chuck, dropping the rope into his hands. He frantically tied it around his saddle horn. Berra shot straight up in the air and flew back at Tarr and Shia. There was no mistaking their orders as they began backing up in unison. The rope went taut as they continued pulling Chuck and Mirka towards them. Finally, Mirka got his back footing, launching him and Chuck onto the flat surface. At last, they stood, the warrior, Berra, and his priceless stallions, firmly and safely on the landing. The horses reared up in pride.

"Berra, that was a close call girl. You have saved us with your quick thinking." Berra, sitting on Shia, flapped her wings in acknowledgment while Tarr and Shia nodded in agreement.

The beetles glowered angrily at the figures across the moat. "Let's go back," barked one of them. We'll track them down in the castle. I can't believe they even tried it. The Queen needs to be informed. Move it… NOW!"

Chuck watched the beetles head back to inform Queen Morphina of their survival. "We must hurry now. Unfortunately, we've been discovered, and things could get out of hand." He looked around and found a small room just inside the castle, off to one side of the entry. He led them in there. "Perfect," he thought.

"Okay, Tarr, with your coloring, you will be hard to make out. Mirka and Shia, we'll be back shortly. If anyone comes near you, you've been in danger before. Spare no one." With that they raced into the castle.

With Berra floating through the air above him, Chuck started the tedious task of searching each room in the dreary castle for Keewae, Kehi, and Porcelain. As they crept down the hall, Berra would sing and draw beetles towards them. The beetles were then cut down by Tarr or skewered by Chuck, thus clearing their path. When they finally reached the same gloomy hallway Keewae and Kehi had vanished into, he heard voices echoing through the chambers, one of which, he was sure, belonged to Queen Morphina. He whispered to Tarr and Berra to wait for him, then crept forward towards a door where the voices were coming from.

He reached a door, tugging it quietly and slowly ajar. He saw the Queen but not her audience.

"...and furthermore, what's a fuzzar and that other Japanese traitor doing in my castle trying to rescue my poor, pathetic Porcelain? How did they manage to get in? Answer me!" she ranted on.

"Why don't you ask Coridon and your hourglass beetles? Where is that evil, wretched creature anyway? How can you be associating with that psychotic beetle after what she did to you and stepmother?"

Chuck pulled the door open slightly more. He could see Keewae tightly bound and placed in a metal cage. He was unconscious and bleeding from his ear. Kehi was nowhere to be found. Then he saw Porcelain. She was in a glass enclosure and seemed to be in bad condition. She was a very pale green and was injured.

"This is a disaster," he thought. He took a big risk and craned his head around the door, spying Dodge near the ceiling perched on a small ledge hidden from their captures.

"I don't know what you are talking about. One thing is obvious," she continued her rant, "someone has been bitten, and you came here to steal my eggs." She whirled on Porcelain. "Why would you risk coming back here after escaping years ago if you weren't helping Princess Salair? I know she was the one who stepped on my red orbus. Hopefully, the poison worked its magic."

Porcelain, abused and weak as she was, still retorted, "Let them go. There is no need for your brutality. I don't care about myself."

"Brutality? You haven't seen anything yet. You and your friends are thieves. You have no right taking any of my eggs."

"By the looks of it, you haven't changed a bit. It's obvious that your heart has only grown harder and darker. But there is still hope for you, can't you see? You still have that turquoise patch by your wings, and if I'm not mistaken, it has gotten bigger."

"No, it hasn't!" Screeched Morphina. "My heart is dark because of what you did to me."

"I've never done anything to you."

"How did my cocoon get damaged then?" Morphina screamed angrily.

"We've been over this a thousand times; your so-called beetle friends smashed into your cocoon. They killed your mother and tried to eat you before you hatched. But father drove them away... You're lucky to still be alive."

"Ha! What a story! I'm sure you believe it too!"

"Of course, I do. Father told it to me."

"You mean my father. You're adopted and would believe anything he told you. He's a liar and you're naive."

"I consider him my father," Porcelain stated stubbornly. "He took me in when I was very little, and don't you dare call him a liar. Even you know better than that. Shame on you!"

The evil, hard-hearted Morphina was ashamed. She hurriedly turned her face from Porcelain and batted back some tears. She knew full well her father would never lie to either one of them.

"No, Samantha, it's the truth. And the irony is, the very ones who tried to destroy you... you consider them your friends. Friends? Really? Like I said, they... were the ones who caused your deformity." Porcelain was weary and sick of this conversation.

"Liar!" Morphina lashed out. "And don't call me Samantha. She doesn't exist anymore. You just want to be the sole heir of the Swallow Kingdom!" Morphina was turning black with anger now.

Porcelain pitied her. "Have you lost your mind? Of course, Samantha exists. I wasn't even around then. You were the heir. Everyone knew it. You just chose to run off like a coward and align yourself with Coridon, the real killer. Don't you find it odd that Coridon poisoned you against father and me? Is this the kind of heir to the throne you envisioned? This vile, dark, disgusting, creepy forest and castle with no family or love?"

"Shut up! I have that here!"

Porcelain persisted. "Really? Look at your surroundings. Do you see anything bright and happy? Who are your friends? Do you consider Coridon your mother now? I hope not. Coridon is your enemy and the quicker you realize that the better off you will be. Remind me again? When was the last time you saw your father?"

"Don't talk to me about father or my family," Morphina shouted.

"Why not? Porcelain asked. "It was bad enough your mother was killed, but you made it worse by being hateful and cruel to him after her death. It was devastating for him, accusing him, not Coridon, of purposely damaging your cocoon. How did your mother get killed, by the way? Did you ever ask Coridon what exactly happened?"

"She told me it would be too painful for me to know. She took me under her wing and cared for me after my mother died."

"Of course she did. To poison you against father, to take over his kingdom. How's that going, by the way? Look around. Look what you are doing and where you are. No kingdom, no family. Coridon is never nice to you anyway, from what I've always witnessed. Your father's the one who always loved you. Coridon doesn't even know what love is. She uses everyone around her."

"You don't know what you're talking about. I'll never go back. Father did not want an ugly, deformed half-butterfly to be his heir! I have never felt like a butterfly anyway. Look at my wing. It's not a butterfly wing. I'm deformed and ugly."

"And that is what Coridon keeps telling you over and over again, isn't it? To keep you down."

Morphina was quiet for a second. For the first time, Porcelain saw sadness and confusion on her stepsister's face.

Truly, the deformed butterfly was deeply troubled and beset with doubts. Then, subconsciously she heard a soft, luring voice quietly urging, "Come to me Morphina, now my dear. Come now."

"I must go now. I'm coming Coridon," she whispered under her breath. She was getting more confused now.

She stood to leave Porcelain's presence, but she was disoriented. For just a moment, she wanted to believe what Porcelain had said, but she made an active effort to squelch that feeling. She couldn't get weak; she must not weaken. That 'turquoise stain' was throbbing now as she winced in pain. Yashi motioned over to Porcelain with her eyes while Porcelain nodded, understanding what Yashi was trying to tell her.

She wanted to get away from Porcelain before she noticed her discomfort.

"As usual, Porcelain, you don't know what you're talking about. Yellowjacket and his killer bees should arrive shortly. I should have taken care of you the first time. His bees will have a field day with you and your friends. See you soon, dear stepsister, or not." She pressed her face against the glass container and grinned at Porcelain before leaving, sending chills up Porcelain's spine.

"Come on Yashi, let's go and make sure the other intruder is still out." Yashi looked like she wanted to die. She didn't want any part of this nastiness. Yashi was a kind butterfly who got caught accidentally one day by Coridon's beetles. Her choice was death or slavery to these two wicked creatures. She chose to be a servant in the hopes of escaping one day. She endured the never-ending cruelty of the two of them. She knew Queen Morphina very well. She knew she didn't want to talk about her turquoise patch because it was the good in her that was trying to push out the evil. Coridon was unaware of this, but Yashi was hopeful that the patch would keep growing. The fact that Morphina even teared up was a very good sign.

Chuck jumped behind the door just as the Queen burst through it, striding briskly down the hall, her guards scrambling to keep up.

Chuck stood still for a moment, the heated but enlightening conversation between the sisters vibrating in his mind. As they disappeared down the corridor, Chuck got Berra and whispered to her, "Follow them and see where they took Oshi. Stay out of sight, girl. Be careful, Berra." Berra, with her feathers turning dark for protection, quietly flapped her wings, rose into the air very close to the ceiling, which was obscured in darkness, and floated after the mad Queen.

Chuck went back and grabbed Tarr. "Let's go boy, we must hurry."

Thinking about the argument between the sisters, Chuck was able to put the pieces of the puzzle together. He thought of Porcelain. With her magical powers and exquisite coloring, the contrast to the deformed, oddly colored stepsister was striking. No wonder she treated Porcelain the way she did. Porcelain reminded her that she had no beauty inside or out. He felt bad for both of them. Porcelain was still trying to save her; however, Morphina had been poisoned against her family, maybe beyond repair.

With the room now empty and no sight of Morphina, Dodge flew to Porcelain's cage. He circled it frantically, trying to figure out a way to get Porcelain out.

"It's okay, Dodge. I'll be okay." Porcelain was crying and clearly distraught when Chuck stepped into the room.

"Porcelain," he whispered, "don't cry. We'll get you out of here." He lifted the heavy glass cage off Porcelain while she drew in a breath of air. "Thank you, Chuck. I wasn't sure if she was trying to suffocate me or not. How did you get in here?"

"Wasn't easy."

"But I thought it was impossible. I thought I had to be with you!"

"Wish you had been; it would have been easier."

"I am so happy to see you, but we must hurry. My sister will be back with Yellowjacket."

Chuck went over to where they had Keewae caged. "Keewae, Keewae." Chuck was shaking him, trying to revive him.

"What? Oh, my head," Keewae said, holding his bloody head. "Where am I? What happened?"

"It was a trap, Keewae. It wasn't your fault," said Porcelain.

"Chuck! You're back. Oh boy. This is really embarrassing."

"We'll talk about your embarrassment later, buddy. We've got to get out of here. Lean back against the cage so Tarr can kick the lock. Dodge, keep a lookout. This will be noisy."

Dodge flew to the door.

"Okay, Tarr, let her rip." Tarr nodded, reared up, and came down with force. The lock didn't budge.

"Again." Still didn't budge. Dodge came flying back in. Tarr gave Dodge a look. Normally, that was not enough to deter Dodge, but he knew Tarr meant business. He looked at Tarr, nodded, and flew back outside to guard the door. Tarr was so irritated with Dodge that he reared up and came down with even more force, breaking the lock.

"Awesome. Let's go. Keewae, you and Porcelain get on Tarr while I lead him out of here."

"Nonsense," Keewae staggered backwards.

"Right, Keewae. Tarr, kneel." Keewae slung his leg over and got on Tarr. Chuck carefully scooped up Porcelain.

"Here you go," he said and handed Porcelain to Keewae. "Dodge, go ahead of us. Find Berra. I know this is not the right time, but I heard you and Morphina talking. Sounds like Coridon has something to do with all this, including her deranged view of what happened to her?"

"Queen Swallow came across Coridon, who was mysteriously hovering over what she thought was Samantha's cocoon. When the Queen tried to stop her, Coridon's beetles engulfed her, killing her and trampling Samantha's cocoon in the process. The King arrived late, finding his wife dead and Samantha's cocoon severely damaged. He did what he could to save Samantha, but she needed to be in her cocoon longer, hence her deformity. She has never accepted this explanation. All she sees is an ugly, deformed butterfly. To answer your question, yes. Unbeknownst to King Swallow, Coridon planted a couple of beetles in Samantha's room. I discovered them one night when I went into her room. I heard whispering and found them. I assume they had been doing this for a while as she slept, whispering lies and filling her head with untruths about how she became deformed. Eventually, her hatred for us became too much. So, she decided to join forces with Coridon and spread her hatred."

Porcelain winced in pain.

"Chuck let's go. We need to get out of here." Keewae was worried about the delicate butterfly.

Porcelain gained strength and continued, "She punishes me for looking like a normal butterfly... while she cannot. My stepfather told her it didn't matter what she looked like; she was still beautiful to him, but she refused to believe him. Coridon had succeeded in poisoning her mind."

"I am sorry, Porcelain, but you're hardly a normal butterfly, in case you hadn't noticed. We can talk about this later. We need to get Oshi and get out of here. Let's go Tarr. What's with the killer bees? Did I hear that correctly?"

"Yes," said Porcelain, "she has sort of an alliance with them."

"What?" asked Keewae, "that is bad news. The sooner we get out of here and away from them, the better."

Berra and Dodge came flying out of the gloom and into sight, landing on Chuck's shoulder. She emitted a sharp cry.

"It's Kehi. Lead the way Berra."

"Dodge, go with Berra," instructed Porcelain.

They made their way down the hall in the darkness, following Berra.

"Porcelain, why haven't we run into any guards? There has to be a bunch of them somewhere, right? Afterall, her beetles saw us jump over the moat. I thought they would be swarming the castle."

"My sister may have thought that more help was coming and placed her guards outside, around the castle. It is a bit odd, however, not that I'm complaining. Just be wary though, as they hide in the walls, so you never know where they are."

"That's the last thing I remembered before we got ambushed," said Keewae.

CHAPTER 31

Morphina stormed down the hall, grateful to have temporarily gotten away from Porcelain. She was still trying to fight back tears, and her turquoise patch felt like it was on fire. She thought to herself, "How could father love me looking like this? Could Porcelain be right? Could father love me anyway? I do miss him, but I'm so ugly. Porcelain is so beautiful. Maybe I will ask Coridon how my mother died. I guess we never talked about it." She wiped away her tears and shuffled down a long, dark hallway, stopping at a metal door, waiting.

"Morphina?"

"Yes, Coridon."

"Come in, darling."

"Wait here," she commanded her guards.

She stepped through the door, not wanting to talk to Coridon about Porcelain's return to her castle. "Coridon, you needed me?"

Coridon was lying in her bed of moss with her servant beetles waiting on her every whim. She was old, crippled and cruel. She was seething at the fact that her beetles were being slain, cutting off the visual surveillance of her forest, and worst of all, Porcelain was in the castle.

"What is your sister doing here? What were you two talking about? She's the reason you are so ugly, remember? You need to get rid of her immediately. I can't see around the forest. Where are my beetles?" Coridon was barking so many questions at Morphina that it was making her patch throb even worse.

"Porcelain said you would know how my mother was killed. She said your beetles did it. Is that true?"

Coridon pushed herself up, leered a dangerously evil stare at Morphina, and growled, "If you ever ask me that again, you will perish. Do I make myself clear?"

Morphina turned ghostly white and stepped backwards.

"Get out."

Morphina hurried out, snapping at her guards.

"Get more of Coridon's beetles out in the field immediately."

"Yes, my Queen." The guards hurried off to carry out their order.

Morphina had seen Coridon in a foul mood before, but she was even worse than usual.

"I shouldn't have questioned her, I guess. Maybe Porcelain was right. Her reaction was not what I expected. She threatened to end my life?" she thought to herself. "She'll be in a better mood once Porcelain is gone and her beetles are restored in the forest."

"Oh ouch," she winced again. The pain coming from her turquoise patch was unbearable, and it seemed like it was growing ever so slightly. "Oh no, this can't be happening. If Coridon sees this, it won't go well for me. Maybe I should take Porcelain's advice and go find father. He'll know what to do." Morphina was sad and confused, with no one to talk to.

CHAPTER 32

"With so much happening, I totally forgot to ask about the Princess. How thoughtless of me. Did you get to her in time?" Porcelain inquired.

"Yes, yes, I did. It was a close call. You saved the Princess, Porcelain. Without those eggs, she would have perished, and she has no one else to thank but you."

"Down here!" cried a beetle.

"Hurry," said Porcelain, "down this hallway." As they made their way down the dark hall, they came to the only locked door. No one said a word while Porcelain studied a couple of bricks on the wall.

"Keewae, lift me over there." He complied as she stretched her leg out, touching one of the bricks, which allowed the door to open.

"This way! They went down here!" said the guard.

"Hurry," said Porcelain as they stepped through the doorway. Immediately, the door closed behind them.

Porcelain was wincing in pain now.

The guards were baffled. All they saw was a gloomy, dusty, deserted hallway with a closed door at the end – a door that, as far as they knew, had been locked and unopened for years.

"They went this way, I swear," insisted one beetle.

"Are you sure about that?" asked the head guard.

"Of course I am."

"Check the door." They went down the hall and tried to open the door but couldn't.

"This door has been locked for as long as I can remember."

"That can't be. I swear I saw them come down here."

"Let's try the next hall. Maybe they went down there," volunteered another guard, pointing to another dark passage in the opposite direction.

Waiting silently and listening anxiously, they breathed a collective sigh of relief. "Whew, that was close," muttered Keewae. "Thank you, Porcelain."

"I need to get to Kehi. You guys keep going. My ponies are at the back entrance to the castle. We'll meet you there."

"That would not be possible, Chuck," said Porcelain. "You don't know your way around in here. And you don't know where the secret bricks are to help you get out. We will wait for you right here."

Berra was sitting on Tarr's saddle, listening to all of it. Chuck noticed Berra staring at him, her feathers taking on a slight glow. A sign that meant he needed to listen to Porcelain.

Chuck knew she was right. Porcelain was suffering from the effects of her capture and injuries. She did not look well, yet she was still helping them.

"Alright," he yielded, "but here's the deal. You stay right here for no more than fifteen minutes. If I have not returned by then, Keewae, you get Porcelain out of here.

Keewae shook his head. "If we must."

Dodge was fluttering around Porcelain, clearly concerned about her well-being. He nodded his head up and down in agreement with Chuck.

"I don't think that is a good idea," objected Porcelain.

"Sorry, Porcelain, but that's the way it is going to be. You have risked your life enough times for us."

"Alright, but hurry back," nodded Porcelain, knowing Chuck was right and she was too weak to be of any help. "Press that brick right there then. Be careful."

Chuck pressed the brick he was told to, and the door once again opened.

"Okay, Berra, let's go. Show me where Oshi is."

Berra glided smoothly along the dim hallway, with Chuck following behind. They reached a small, closed door. Berra hovered above it and gave a barely audible chirp. Chuck found the latch, opened the door, and spied his longtime friend. He was lying motionless on the ground, mouth gagged, hands chained and linked to another set of chains around his ankles. He had a bloody gash on the back of his head.

"Come, Berra," he said as he stepped in, closing the door carefully behind him. He rushed over to Oshi and rolled him over to see his face. He was brutally beaten. "Must have been a bunch of them," he thought.

"Oshi," whispered Chuck. He didn't move. Berra flew over to Oshi and landed on his chest. She bent over him and whistled a long, low note.

Kehi's eyes blinked, then remained open. Chuck looked over at Berra who just closed her eyes and nodded to Chuck. "What in the world?" he thought to himself as Kehi took a minute to get his bearings.

"What a sight for sore eyes," he stated. "Let's get out of here, Chuck, and I can explain my stupidity for landing myself in this predicament at another time."

"You were ambushed, Oshi, nothing to say. We need to get these chains off you," said Chuck. He then pulled out a small knife and worked the locks off, binding his friend.

"Where are Porcelain and Keewae?"

"They are waiting for us, but we best hurry."

"Let's go." Berra led them back through the darkness and found the others again.

They reached the door in no time.

"Porcelain, it's us," whispered Chuck.

"They're back!" whispered Porcelain. "Keewae press the brick again please."

"Okay, Porcelain, one more errand. We have to get Shia and Mirka. They are waiting for us near the back entrance."

"That's where we are headed anyway, Chuck. We'll follow you, and then I'll lead the way."

They retrieved Mirka and Shia, dodging the guards along the way, and proceeded to follow Porcelain down another hallway.

"This way," she said, pointing ahead. "Left here." They followed behind. The ground started sloping downwards. "Just keep going."

"Boy, this is getting a little steep," said Keewae as there were no steps, and the path was getting more and more slippery.

"Almost there," said Porcelain. "Okay, stop here. See that mortar hook down there?" she asked Chuck.

"Yes," replied Chuck.

"Turn it to the right."

"Okay!" As he turned the hook, he said, "Okay, what now, Porcelain?"

"Oh no," said Keewae, "Chuck, she has passed out."

As Chuck moved the lever, bricks started disappearing until they left a doorway in front of them.

"Wow, how is she doing all this?" whispered Keewae.

"I have no idea, but this is nothing but an empty room," said Kehi.

"A dead end?" Chuck stated.

"It can't be," said Keewae, "she wouldn't lead us down this path with no escape. Let's hurry, as this may not stay open for long, and I don't want to be standing out here exposed."

"Good point," said Kehi.

Once they all entered the empty room, the bricks reformed, closing everyone inside.

Keewae dismounted and left Porcelain on Tarr.

"I suggest we start looking around for an opening of some kind or something out of place. You know what I mean," suggested Keewae.

Just then, Berra chirped and flew over and landed on Tarr. Berra's feathers took on a glow again as she leaned over Porcelain and waited. The outline of Porcelain's wings began to glow, which stirred Porcelain awake. She then began whispering something to Berra.

"What in the world?" pondered Kehi as they all just waited and watched.

"I don't know," said Chuck. "These two seem to have a mysterious connection." Berra flew over to one corner of the room and started scratching the floor.

"What is it, girl?" They went to the corner. "Let me help, Berra," Chuck insisted. He got down on his knees and started scooping dirt away from the area where Berra was scratching.

"Incredible!" exclaimed Kehi. They had unearthed a bright turquoise stone illuminating the corner.

Once again, Berra flew over and landed on Tarr. She leaned over Porcelain, but she wasn't moving. Berra looked at Chuck and chirped.

"What, girl? I don't understand."

Berra looked at the stone and then at Porcelain.

"I don't... "

"Maybe she wants you to take Porcelain over to the stone?" said Kehi.

Chuck lifted Porcelain off Tarr and set her down by the stone. Porcelain stretched her wing out and touched the stone. Everyone watched as the stone turned into water and then noticed that her wing had briefly turned into some sort of a fin and back again.

"Did you see that?" Cried Kehi.

"I most certainly did!" responded Chuck. "I can't believe my eyes. Was that a fin there for a minute? Did we see that right?"

"That's what it looked like to me," said Keewae. As they all stood there in disbelief, the cave walls began glowing a bright turquoise. Even the turquoise ring of feathers around Berra's neck was now glowing.

"Chuck, look!" Kehi said in amazement.

"What? What? I don't understand any of this!" Chuck said totally dumbfounded, looking at Berra.

"What is that noise?" inquired Kehi.

"I don't know, but it sounds like a rushing river. It is, and it's filled with... ah... are those piranhas?" cried Chuck.

"Majikayo! Piranhas they are!" exclaimed Kehi.

They all stood in the middle of the room while roaring waters filled with piranhas encircled them.

Everyone was mesmerized by what they were witnessing—the changing stone, the rushing waters, the man-eating fish, and then, a flash of light and utter darkness. As their eyes adjusted, they noticed that the wall in front of them had disappeared. They were standing outside the castle once again. Kehi scanned the area for any beetles that may have been waiting but discovered they were further away from the castle than would seem possible.

"Chuck, we're clear from the castle by about a hundred yards?"

Chuck looked around. "Whoa. You're right. She has done it again. Impossible to believe."

"Piranhas, why piranhas," muttered Keewae.

"Porcelain?" Chuck said as he looked over at Porcelain, who was unconscious, with Berra and Dodge standing on each side of her in full protection mode. She let out a few short but high alarming notes.

"Right, Berra, Keewae, we need to get to your friend, and now. We can't afford to lose Porcelain."

"I think that magical feat just sapped the last ounce of strength out of her. Let's go," said Keewae.

They all saddled up and headed to get help for Porcelain.

CHAPTER 33

The Queen and Nia left the servant quarters and walked across the clearing toward the edge of the forest.

"Come with me, Nia. We must hurry before they discover you're missing. But... before we go ahead, I need to tell you something," said the Queen. "I am your mother. Shift kidnapped you soon after you and your sister were born."

"What... but... I knew father was acting weird and hiding something. But you are my mother... The Queen... I am a princess? I have a sister?" Nia stated, shocked.

"I know this is too much to process right now, but I will tell you everything. We don't have much time now, we must get to the trees," the Queen said and disappeared behind thick shrubbery.

Nia, still in disbelief, paused to look back at the castle, which held so many brutal memories. As she gazed upon it, the back door opened, and Prince Drouck strolled through, pacing around, still fuming about Nia's betrayal. He happened to glance in her direction and saw her.

"Nia, what are you doing!" screamed Drouck. "You'll never get out of this forest alive!" Panicked, he screamed, "Guards!" Drouck's eyes turned immediately red. He was now out of his mind with rage. "You have betrayed me for the last time!" He stormed into the castle while the guards streamed out.

"Oh no! Quickly, Nia."

"I shouldn't have stopped. I'm so stupid. I'm so sorry!" Nia said.

"It's okay. Hurry, Nia." The Queen said while grabbing her daughter's hand. "They won't catch us. There is a cave up here ahead of us. Hopefully, the manras haven't found it yet." She raced toward the cavern where Salair and the Colonel were waiting for them.

Neither stopping nor speaking, they ran steadily through the majestic trees, Nia trusting completely in her newly discovered parent. At long last, when the former servant girl thought her lungs would burst, she heard her mother's welcome voice.

"Ah, here it is!" She slowed to a walk and approached some tall shrubbery. "Here Nia, help me erase our tracks." She broke a leafy branch off a nearby tree, and Nia did the same. They strode some distance back and began dragging their branches across their footprints as they returned and entered the cave.

Guards were swarming every which way. They walked right by the cave opening and stopped. "See anything?" asked one manra.

"No. It's starting to get dark, and besides, she'll never make it out alive with all the nasty creatures roaming around at night. Stupid girl. I'll tell the Prince we'll search first light."

"He's not going to like that."

"No, but he knows we can't be out here after dark. Let's go."

The Queen and Nia were holding onto each other while trying to catch their breath. The Queen stuck her head out and watched the manras return to the camp.

"I'm glad we covered our tracks," Nia confessed shakily.

"So am I. Thankfully, they know nothing about this cave."

"That guard was right. There are nasty creatures about to come out."

"We'll be out of here before that. I have help this time."

"What kind of help?"

"Let's see if the manras are gone. Our friends are waiting for us."

"I don't understand any of this."

"I don't expect you to right now. Let's go."

They peered out of the cave.

"I think they're gone," whispered the Queen. She grabbed Nia's hand and ran for Raspin's trees. "There they are. This way, Nia."

"There... what are?"

"Not so fast," a voice said behind them.

"Guys," yelled a manra, "over here! Aghhhh!" as a giant branch swatted away the manra like a pesky fly.

"Whoa!" cried Nia.

"Get on daughter, quickly," the Queen said as the deadly branch waited for them to climb on.

The guards came running up only to watch the Queen and Nia being raised towards the sky and disappear into the trees.

"Did you see that?" cried the guard.

"That's impossible. Follow them."

As soon as they started running after the Queen, shoots from the trunk of Raspin's trees appeared, slapping the manras down. "Ouch!" cried the guards, looking down at their bloody arms. "We need more men!" They said as they headed away from the trees to gather more manras.

"Run, Nia!" The Queen knew the trees could not stay much longer as they had been found out.

"Right behind you," Nia said as she raced behind the Queen across the same bridge Raspin's trees made for the Queen earlier.

The Queen looked back and saw the bridge and trees dissolving behind them. "Oh no. Faster, Nia. Don't look back."

Nia couldn't help it and glanced behind her. "What in the world?"

The bridge was closing in on them. Just as they neared the end, the branches gave way, leaving the Queen and Nia falling from the sky.

"Gotcha!" Raspin grabbed them both with his tree roots and set them down. "That was close, my Queen."

"Yes, Raspin. I'm sorry we ran into a few problems and got delayed. I hope we haven't put you in danger."

"No, my trees have safely disappeared. I am the last one. Your daughter is safe, I see. Cottonwood will be relieved to hear this news."

"Well, I know you must leave, but this is my daughter, Nia, whom you helped save today. Nia, this is my newly found friend, Raspin."

"I don't know what just happened here, but thank you, Raspin, for saving her Highness, I mean, my mother and me. It is an honor to meet you."

"Time is of the essence for both of us, my Queen. I will tell Cottonwood you are safe for now." Before the Queen could respond, Raspin was gone.

"Wow, this is all so unusual and surreal. Who's Cottonwood?"

"I'll explain everything later. We better get out of this area before it's too late. We have little sunlight left. Oh, by the way, you will need this. The Queen handed Nia a porcelain ball to carry. Do not let go of this. It will be your best friend."

"Ah… okay? I think?"

"Follow me."

"Yes ma'am."

Prince Drouck and his men returned to where Raspin's trees used to be. "Where are those so-called trees?" demanded Drouck.

"They were right here! I swear, Your Highness."

"Yes," said the other guard, "I swear too. But… now they are gone!"

"Something very funny is going on around my forest. Search the area. I am going back to The Dark Forest. Keep me updated on your progress. I want her found and brought back here. Nobody escapes me. Understand? First, the Queen and now Nia. I don't know what you and your men are doing, but your incompetence won't be tolerated again. Find her!!" Drouck screamed and stormed off, feeling disgusted with his army and being betrayed by Nia.

"Yes, sir. We will not fail you."

"Seth, let's get the horses and our best tracker. We'll leave a sparse number of guards at the castle. We cannot fail the Prince. You know what will happen to us."

"Hurry, Nia! Unfortunately, because of our tardiness, Raspin had to leave us a little short of the clearing. We must get there immediately." The Queen grabbed Nia's hand, and they started running. They had about thirty yards to go when Nia's hand was ripped out of her own. The Queen whirled around to see a large furry octospy wrapping its leg around Nia's ankle and trying to pull her back into the forest.

"Oh no, you don't!" She grabbed the porcelain ball, and true to form, it transformed into a samurai sword. She took a mighty swing and severed its leg from Nia's ankle. The nasty creature screamed in agony.

"Get away from her!"

"Ouch!" she said as she shoved the severed leg off her ankle, revealing a bloody rash. "Oh, my leg! Ow!"

"That looks bad Nia. But not as bad as what is heading towards us. Here, let me help you. Hurry! We can make it." The Queen hoisted Nia up, but she could barely put any weight on her leg. "Oh, my leg, it hurts really bad."

The Queen put Nia's arm around her neck and scooped her around the waist so they could basically run on three legs. "Come Nia, they are closing on us."

"I can make it," Nia said, groaning in pain.

"You'll never make it," hissed the octospy as they closed in on them. The Queen looked back and saw the octospy right on their heels.

"Faster, Nia." The Queen was practically dragging her towards the sunlit clearing. She looked again over her shoulder just in time to see a giant furry arm right above her head.

"Oh no, you don't!" screamed the Queen. With all her might, she launched herself into the air, carrying Nia with her, and landed hard into the clearing. Nia wrapped up in her arms, rolling over and over, away from the outstretched tentacles into the light. The sunlight hit the octospy, sending it screeching in agony back to the forest.

"Next time," it hissed, "next time!"

She stared back at the forest with shivers running down her spine.

"What are those things?"

"They are called octospy. Very nasty and deadly, as you just saw. Let me see your ankle."

Her ankle was blistered with black poison starting to creep up her leg.

"We need to get you to Misa quickly." All she could think about was Sleet, and she was scared.

"Who's Misa?"

"Our friend, the fuzzar's niece. Misa is just amazing. She helped me when we got to their den. She's sort of a chemist/herbologist and the one who created these weapons we just used."

"Well, I think she just saved our lives."

"Yes, she seems to keep doing that, unbeknownst to her."

Nia bent over in pain, "I hope she can help me. My foot seems to be getting numb."

"Here, put your arm around me. It's not horribly far from here. Let's try to stay close to the forest edge in case Drouck's manras show up."

Nia was in extreme pain now, but there was nothing she could do but bear it.

"It's just ahead... up there, we must hurry," the Queen said, trying to encourage her.

"Okay, can we stop for just a second?" bending over in pain again.

The Queen was nervous. She didn't want to stop, but Nia was in extreme pain.

"Nia, we cannot stop. Your ankle needs immediate attention, trust me. I know you are suffering, but we must go."

"Come back here!" shouted a voice.

"What? Oh no! Where did they come from?" The Queen looked around and saw three manras running after them.

"This is going to be painful, Nia, but we have no choice."

They raced ahead as fast as Nia could stand. "It's around this corner. Hurry Nia! See that leaf wall straight ahead; we are going to dive through it. You must trust me."

Nia was in so much pain she didn't care if it was a brick wall.

"Now!" Cried the Queen. She and Nia dove through the leaf wall and disappeared.

"Let's go. I saw them around this corner. They can't get away now!" cried one of the manras.

All three stopped short, "They were right here. Where'd they go?"

"That's impossible. They're gone," hissed the other manra.

"They must be here. Let's take a look."

Once again, the leaves engulfed the Queen and Nia. Corga and Sin Sin were standing over them. "Don't move," Corga said, pressing his claw into the Queen's back. "Corga, is that you?"

"Queen Victoria? Help me, Sin Sin." They quickly brushed away the leaves, revealing the Queen and Nia.

"My Queen, it is you. Thank the stars! Please forgive me; we had no idea it was you. Here, let me help you up." Sin Sin offered a paw.

"Thank you. You're forgiven," she said, relieved. Nia was now sobbing in pain.

"Is this Nia? You found her!" exclaimed Sin Sin.

"Yes. I'm afraid during our escape, an octospy got hold of her ankle."

"Come with me, Nia. Misa will know how to help you." Sin Sin picked her up like a sack of potatoes and ran to the mud elevator.

"I'm sorry Corga, but we may have company. We thought we were in the clear, but three manras tracked us down. I'm afraid they are snooping around your wall."

"Let's get you to safety. Sin Sin and I will take care of them. Come with me, my Queen. I'm so relieved to see you. We must get word to the King that you are safe."

Corga took Nia down the mud elevator and immediately returned up top with Sin Sin. They could hear voices coming from the other side of their deadly leaf wall. The fur-like tentacles were swirling on the top of their heads in alarm.

"They have to be here. There's nowhere else to go."

"Maybe they went through this leafy area." He stepped through and disappeared.

"Where did he go? Did you see that? He just disappeared."

"I don't like this one bit. What just happened?"

Corga and Sin Sin were waiting for the unsuspecting manra, engulfing him in leaves.

"What do we have here, Corga?" inquired Sin Sin.

"A foolish manra," Corga replied.

"Who are you?" he yelled. "My men are on the other side. Let me up. You have no idea who you're messing with." There was no reply from the other manras. Corga and Sin Sin smiled at each other.

"Elevator, Corga?"

"Excellent idea, brother."

The leaves began to swirl, picking up the manra with them. Corga and Sin Sin headed to the mud elevator with the captured manra in tow.

"What's going on?!! Help me! Ahhhhhhh!" muffled cries came from the leaf-bound prisoner.

The screams continued until the elevator door closed.

"Did you hear something? Was that screaming?"

"I don't like this. Can you hear anything?" they stepped towards the leafy area to get a closer look. They got a little too close for comfort for Corga and Sin Sin, who yanked them through the wall, where, yet again, the leaves and the elevator made short work of the unsuspecting manras.

“Hopefully, those were the only three that were stupid enough to venture into our den,” sighed Sin Sin. “Why don’t we go check around just to make sure? After all, the Queen is back, and she demands our utmost protection.”

“Agreed, brother. Let’s check the perimeter.”

CHAPTER 34

Seth took a team of manras and his best tracker to find Nia. Thankfully, Drouck only saw Nia, so they had no idea the Queen had come back for her.

"Look here," Ryder said as he bent over to examine some tracks. "There are two sets of tracks here. Nia had help escaping."

"Good work, Ryder," commented Seth. "Where do they lead?"

Ryder kept walking. "Something must have happened."

"What do you mean?"

"It looks like there was some sort of struggle. Look. The footprints stop, and the ground is smooth, like someone was dragged backwards. And look here, only one set of footprints is right next to the person being dragged." He stood there for a moment and looked around. "Over here," he said as he spotted more of their tracks. "So, someone must have gotten hurt because these footprints are side by side."

"What do you mean by that, Ryder?"

"I mean, if you can't walk very well, someone would be helping you walk, right?"

"I see!" A sly smile came across Seth's face. "Someone is wounded, and that would mean their escape would be slowed down."

"It would be."

"Keep going, Ryder. We'll follow you, but let's speed up a bit."

Ryder picked up his pace, scanning and zigzagging the ground before him. He came to a stop again.

"Seth, over here. Our men must have been chasing them. Three sets of footprints right here," Ryder stated, pointing in front of him.

"Where the heck did they go?"

"Follow me," stated Ryder. "They can't be far. These footprints are too fresh."

CHAPTER 35

Corga and Sin Sin made their way outside their den, past the leaf barrier, and around the corner into the forest.

"Corga," whispered Sin Sin as he pointed ahead. They crouched down to watch Seth and his men making their way closer to their den.

"We better get back. We can't risk being seen and lead them anywhere near our den," replied Corga.

"Agreed."

They crept back towards their den. As they left the forest's edge and entered their area, trees started rising out of the ground behind them. Tall, thick, mighty trees. "Are you seeing what I'm seeing, Corga?" When they stopped, the trees stopped.

"It's like they are following us and putting up a wall of protection."

"You're right, ah, I hope. Let's get home, brother."

They reached their den and watched the trees continue their path all the way to the other edge of the forest so as to not have a suspicious gap.

"I don't understand what is going on, Corga, but I welcome whatever it is."

"I agree. This is unbelievably peculiar. I have never seen anything like that. Out of the blue, a protective wall. We'll have to ask Uncle about that."

"Let's go check on the Queen and Nia."

CHAPTER 36

"Anything, Ryder?"

"All the footprints are still heading in this direction. Keep going, Seth. They have to be right ahead." Ryder started jogging, keeping the footprints in sight. He rounded the corner and headed towards Keewae's den, stopping at the newly formed tree line.

"That's not possible. Where did they go?" He searched back and forth.

"What's the problem, Ryder? Where are they?" Seth was getting agitated now.

"I don't know. The tracks lead right up to these trees. It couldn't be more obvious."

"I don't care what could be more obvious. Are we supposed to tell the Prince that?" snapped Seth. "Their tracks must be around here. You just lost them."

"I didn't, Seth. Look for yourself."

He dismounted his stallion and stormed over to Ryder. "Look Seth, see the three manra tracks go here. They followed Nia and whoever she was with. All tracks lead to these trees, and they just end here."

"Men, dismount and bring your axes. We'll just cut through one of these trees and find out."

"I don't know about that, Seth. This row of trees looks like a giant gate. A gate not to be reckoned with."

"Maybe, but there is no way through it unless we chop down an opening. You said the tracks end here, so they have to be on the other side, right?"

"Yes, but I have a bad feeling. I don't think that is a good idea."

"Look Ryder, Nia is on the other side of this wall, gate, whatever you want to call it, and we aren't leaving here without her. Dare I say we can't go back without her. Now swing away men."

The first manra took a giant swing into the tree. The sharp blade barely nicked the mighty trunk.

"It will take more than that," snapped Seth.

"I know, sir, but the axe is stuck," replied his soldier as he was trying to pry the axe back out for another whack.

"Give me an axe." Seth stepped up and swung away, landing another blow with the same result.

"I told you, Seth," Ryder said as he was backing away. "Something is not right. Chopping down a tree is not that hard."

"Shut up, Ryder. Everyone else, get your axes. Try another tree." As they started towards their horses, a loud crack thundered above them. The ground below their feet rumbled in furor.

"Let's get out of here!" shouted one of the manras as they all started to run. It was too late. Like a giant lasso, the trees engulfed the small, helpless army of manras and disappeared underground, expunging everyone in their wake.

CHAPTER 37

Chuck was holding onto Porcelain as they rode with Keewae to his 'friend's house'. Porcelain wasn't moving, and the beautiful turquoise butterfly had turned a pale green. Chuck was worried that he was going to lose her. Berra, sitting on Chuck's shoulder, glanced down occasionally and then over to Chuck, worried about her friend. It made Chuck feel even worse. On the other hand, Dodge was flying around back and forth and then landing, staring at Porcelain, then taking off again. He didn't know what to do with himself.

"Dodge, come here," said Kehi holding out his arm for Dodge to land. "You're not helping anyone. Settle down." Dodge flew over and rested with Kehi, knowing he was worrying everyone.

"Nothing will happen to her, I promise."

"Are we close to getting to your friend, Keewae? Porcelain is not doing too well."

"It's not much further. Just down this way."

"Your friend lives in this part of the forest? Isn't this still a dangerous area?" Chuck was getting a bit alarmed, as in front of them lay an ominous, dark path engulfed in a web of giant gnarled fossilized stems.

"It's dangerous Chuck; you are right. She stays in this area for a reason," replied Keewae.

"She?" asked Kehi.

"Keewae, what's going on? Who is your so-called friend?"

Keewae sighed, "This is highly, highly secretive."

They waited.

"My friend is The Rose Fairy."

"The Rose Fairy?" Chuck stopped dead in his tracks. "The one that presides over the Ancient Dynasty, that Rose Fairy? She's in this forest under everyone's nose?"

"Yes Chuck, that very same Ancient Dynasty."

"Very clever," said Kehi, "what better way to hide yourself."

"How is it that you know her?"

"It's a long story, Chuck. A story for later. Let's go now. We must save Porcelain."

The Trilogy continues...

www.ingramcontent.com/pod-product-compliance
Lightning Source LLC
Chambersburg PA
CBHW070632310726
48982CB00001B/261
9798992415513